SKULL JUGGLER

DISENCHANTED

Natalia Locatelli

PUBLISHED BY:

Skull Juggler Publishing
Address: 8101 Biscayne Boulevard, Suite 516, Miami, FL 33138, USA
For internet book purchases or bulk orders, please visit:
www.SkullJuggler.com

This book was printed in the United States of America.

ISBN Softcover: 978-1-933437-15-6
ISBN E-Book: 978-1-1933437-16-3
LCCN: 2008905672

© MMVIII by Natalia Locatelli

All rights reserved. No part of this book may be reproduced or transmitted in any form or by any means, electronic, or mechanical, including photocopying, recording, or by any information storage and retrieval system, without permission in writing from the copyright owner.

Cover and Interior Design by:

Prime Concepts Group Publishing (PCG)
Website: www.PrimeConcepts.com
Cover design: Jeff Sparks, PCG
Interior design: Chad Fatino, PCG

We thank Keshua Orisme from D.I.V.A Photography Inc. at www.MemoriesByDiva.com for Natalia Locatelli's pictures.

Acknowledgements

Many (sometimes unsuspecting) people helped me get this book finished, including but not limited to my parents, my friends, and various adults and teachers throughout my academic career.

I would like to thank my various readers, including Catherine Greene and my fanfiction fans who have followed me for at least five years now. You guys are absolutely amazing, wonderful people. Thank you so much for helping me with this huge project! And a big thank you to Debbie Liebross and Christine Dardet for their amazing energy. You inspired me without even knowing it.

I want to thank my family: my dad, my amazing uncle, my little bro, my family in Argentina. I especially want to thank my mom for getting this book off the ground through her persistence, her big ideas, her generous nature, and her commitment to getting my dreams accomplished my way. Thank you everyone who told me to ignore everyone else's advice and just do what I knew I had to do.

I also have to thank the inspirational teachers I've

had at the University of Miami, especially Professor Debra Dean and Professor Eugene Clasby for helping me remember how much I love writing. And of course all the writers that have inspired me – I'm sure there are hints of them lurking in these pages.

Lastly, I have to thank my boyfriend, Andrew. Thank you for leaving the country for a month and a half so I could finish this project (haha, just kidding, I really missed you). And thank you also for reading through one of my many drafts. If it wasn't for your sometimes painful honesty, this book would literally suck.

Dedication

To my mom, for pushing me even when I'd given up. To my dad, who knew all along that I'd make it to the finish line, one way or the other.

To my friends, who inspired me when my parents couldn't, especially my boyfriend.

To Ms. Greene, who taught me how to write stories properly, and who I never could have done this without. This book is especially for you.

Table of Contents

Chapter 1 – The Wake 11

    Interlude – The Death Festivities 31

Chapter 2 – The Funeral 33

    Interlude – The First Necromancer 47

Chapter 3 – The Deal 49

    Interlude – The Black Roses 63

Chapter 4 – Last Rites 67

    Interlude – The Three Princesses 83

Chapter 5 – The Mourners 87

    Interlude – Rosemary Seeds: A Love Story 103

Chapter 6 – Revenge 111

    Interlude – The Tin Shoes 121

Chapter 7 – The Last Breath 125

    Interlude – The Widow's Lake 133

- Chapter 8 – Escape 137
  - Interlude – The Book of Horn – "The Act" 147
- Chapter 9 – Home 153
  - Interlude – Untitled 161
- Chapter 10 – The Struggle 163
  - Interlude – The Bill of Freedom: Preamble 183
- Chapter 11 – The Safe Haven 185
  - Interlude – The Book of Horn – "Zombies" 203
- Chapter 12 – Memories 207
  - Interlude – The Disenchanted King 225
- Chapter 13 – Disenchanted 227
  - About The Author 241

Nobody knows, in fact, what death is, nor whether to man it is perchance the greatest of all blessings.

- Socrates, 4th Century, B.C.

- I -
The Wake

He came to court on one of the most memorable nights of my life, in the days following the death of my father. This man was a magician, a horrible death sorcerer. Some called him an evil spirit, others called him the Angel of Death, but when I first met him he was called the Skull Juggler. I came to regard him as my friend, although that was not until much later.

The first time I met him was a night of strange happenings. The night was cold and the sky was pregnant with rain that would not fall. The air was filled with a tension that the animals felt, especially the birds as they restlessly darted from roof to roof, cawing at each other in total disharmony. That particular day I was trapped, as always, in my room. Also typical, I was with my mathematics tutor, Gilbert Humms, a man who made even the most fascinating topic mind-numbingly boring. To keep myself awake, I stared out the window at the birds as they flitted across the sky, noticing their strange behavior through a haze of laziness.

I remember feeling angry with Mother for forcing this new kind of torture upon me. What could I possibly use it for? A king doesn't need math if he has a treasurer, I grumbled to myself, and what hope do I have of even being good at it when my professor is so incomprehensible?

I was half lying, half sitting at my desk, ignoring his ramblings as he argued with himself over some mathematical quandary that lead him in an endless circle of discussion. He too seemed to have forgotten that I was in the room as he rambled on and on. I had sketched a rough list of things he said: "simply incomprehensible," "utterly incongruent," and "nullifying quandary" just to name a few. I'd made a check list of how often he said each phrase, discovering with some surprise that "nullifying quandary" seemed to be his absolute favorite term. I mentally applauded his creativity in sneaking this phrase repeatedly into his lecture, musing that he must practice in front of the mirror every morning to get it just right.

Normally I would have at least feigned interest, but this was impossible. How could I concentrate on the man when he was droning on about "hellish decimals" and "peculiar linear rhythms"? Despite my attempts at humor and amusement, I had other things to think about.

My father had died only a week or so ago, murdered in the most horrendous fashion I could conceive of. I flinched from the memory of his funeral, concentrating on the professor's words to distract me. It didn't work. I could see the men-at-arms carrying his body on a great marble slab, shuffling ominously through a crowd of mourners. I remembered staring wide-eyed at the procession, the sound strangely dulled as I watched. I knew peripherally that people were sobbing and I knew that my arm should have hurt from my mother's hand clenched so tightly around my wrist, but I didn't hear or feel anything. I felt numb, watching the procession as if from a long way away.

Something, some feeling in the pit of my stomach, made me wake up. I took a quick peek out of my window, gazing out over the tops of pine trees surrounding the castle, out over the indigo sky and the colony of stars clustered at the horizon. Then I lowered my gaze to the edge of the forest, to the gray ground where the grass was dying from lack of rain. The worn path leading away from the castle was populated as it never was with newcomers from foreign lands.

Carriages poured into the dirt lane, all in various colors and designs, all with their horses dressed in the livery of the various noble families. I could make out some of the coat-of-arms on the doors and roofs of each carriage, mentally checking off each one as I saw it go by. I could see the indigo and silver of House Rannoch, the canary-yellow and orange of House Imago, and the scarlet and gray of House Nerada. These houses were all closely tied to my family through generations of history, all come to pay their respects to my dead father.

Today was the first day of the death festivities. All the people I'd ever known (and didn't know) came to dance, cheer, get drunk, and celebrate in honor of my father and his prosperous rule. A party was the last thing on my mind, since I was probably the only one who cared that my father was dead. I missed him a great deal. I had loved him and respected him and I knew that more than half of my horrible guests came merely to celebrate and not to commemorate him as a ruler. As cynical as I was, I'd hoped that I might have some time to mourn before the circus came to the castle.

As these annoyed thoughts passed through my mind, I saw him for the first time. There wasn't anything special about him, looking down from a great distance. He was not particularly eye-catching from where I was, nor did he have a particularly remarkable carriage. There was just something about the way he stood, watching the passing horses with his arms crossed over his chest, the way he seemed to move about, that caught my eye.

At that moment he raised his eyes to stare at me, stepping out from the shadow of his black carriage. He shouldn't have been able to see me with all the enchantments and architectural obstacles in the way and I shouldn't have been able to see him in such detail through the darkness overhead. I did see him, though, and I knew instinctively that he saw me and was aware of my eyes watching him. He was dressed all in black with a mask shaped like a skull covering his face, his elegant black hair smoothed back seamlessly down his cloaked back. He looked more like a raven than a man, with his long hooked nose and his piercing eyes. His white-gloved hands peeked out of his cloak, the personification of ease. Some nagging voice in the back of my head told me to watch and remember him, that he would be important somehow.

As I pondered this utterly ridiculous sentiment, Mathew Ingram (my personal advisor), Armand Grode (my tailor), and Mother entered my chambers. The room immediately became cramped and claustrophobic, drawing my attention away from the man in black. Mother exchanged some eloquent words with my professor, who seemed particularly flabbergasted by her appearance, before she approached me. Mathew quietly ushered Professor Gilbert out of the room, soothing him with various nonsense.

"Christopher, what are you doing still learning your mathematics," Mother demanded, dramatically flinging her person across the room towards me. I rolled my eyes, too accustomed to her dramatics to appreciate them.

"Mother, you were the one who sent him to my room to-," I began.

"I don't care, Christopher," she said, smoothing invisible wrinkles on her vibrant golden dress. She was ready for the party, I could see. She'd even done her hair in the latest fashion, something she had not done for a while. "You only have two minutes in which to dress for the ball. Why are you wasting time when you know your guests will be waiting for you? You should know better." She looked around my room as she spoke, a frown on her face. I could see her criticism of my room without needing to say a word. I moved around the table and walked to my closet, keeping my expression as emotionless as possible.

"I'll be ready in one minute," I said curtly. Armand, already pulling out some extra pins from his sleeve, attempted to follow me but I waved him away, deliberately slamming the door behind me. I heard Mathew sigh loudly once he thought I was gone. I pressed my ear to the door, holding my breath.

"The boy has no discipline since his father grew ill,"

I heard Mother growl. Mathew cleared his throat as he shuffled about. He hated to be reminded of my sour disposition since my father's death and often knew just what to say to get Mother off his back.

"He will be dealt with, my lady," he said in his high-pitched voice. I could picture him perfectly just by listening to his voice. His long salt and pepper beard twitched whenever he spoke, which gave him the appearance of having a much larger chin than he really did. Those dark brown eyes were usually hidden by his gray hair, which he kept stylishly combed forward to hide the fact that he was balding. He was younger than he pretended to be and often criticized my actions when he thought I wasn't listening in his attempts to people-please. He was not my favorite person in the world.

"Give the boy some space," Armand's soothing voice came from right next to my door, "he has had a difficult ordeal with his father's death. We should be thankful he hasn't done anything more drastic."

"I suppose you're right," Mother's voice said farther away.

"Let us hope it remains that way," Mathew said ominously. I scowled at the door, wishing I could hit him (not for the first time).

When I heard the door to my room close as the adults left and no other sounds in my room, I quickly discarded my day clothes and slipped into my evening attire. I chose my onyx crown instead of my usual gold circlet, although it felt heavy and uncomfortable on my head. It had been my father's favorite crown and this was an event for him. I wanted to laugh at myself.

It was fashionable to be in mourning in my kingdom. It was an excellent excuse to wear nothing but black every day. The only ones who hadn't been wearing black for the past week were the servants, who only wore black armbands over their usual servant uniforms. Everyone else, all of the guests who stayed in the various guest rooms, drifted through the halls wearing the most decorative black outfits they could find, usually with touches of color here and there like a gold shawl or a red pair of shoes. It was eye-catching on purpose and nauseating at the same time. They'd made my father's death a fashion statement.

Despite this trend, wearing black at a formal party was not socially acceptable. I wanted to make an impression on my guests, so I ignored this unspoken decree. Everyone else could be merry and ignorant, but I wasn't going to pretend everything was all fun and games. I knew what the party was supposed to be about.

As I exited my closet, the guards on either side of the door stiffened their posture. Armand stood beside my door and grinned as I came out. He motioned to my guards to relax, which they did instantly. Armand was something of a power figure at the castle – nearly everyone listened to him. Even I relaxed as I approached him and let a scowl show through my usual emotionless mask. He laughed when he saw the expression on my face.

"Don't tell me you're going to the party dressed like that. Your mother will have a fit," he said with an amused smile.

"She'll have a fit anyway when she finds out how

badly I've been doing in my mathematics lately," I said petulantly. Armand went into the closet and retrieved a flowing black cape with ermine fur lining around the neck and a red underside. I scowled at it but allowed Armand to put it over my shoulders and adjust it properly. He hummed softly as he did, making me relax against my will.

"Try not to get yourself into trouble tonight," he said softly. "There are many friends among you, but there are just as many enemies. You are only protected so long as you remain close to those who can care for you." I could feel him look over my shoulder to the guards standing on either side of the only door. These two men were only part of the larger King's Guard, expressly trained in close-quarters combat. Their swords were dipped in red widow's poison and their arrows were sharpened so finely that they could pierce armor from great distances. I knew what Armand was trying to say, as he'd always hinted this idea to me since I was old enough to understand. There were people who did not want me on the throne and only those who I could trust would protect me from them.

I nodded absently, thinking about how no one had been around when my father needed protecting. Armand seemed to understand what was on my mind since he patted my shoulder affectionately and nudged me towards the door. "We'll have an after party in the servants' quarters whenever you're free from your obligations. We hope to see you there," he said.

"There had better be a great deal of alcohol when

I get there," I said with a grin. The guards opened the door, bowing as I walked past them.

They followed me down the stairs towards the main study. I opened the secret passage leading into the corridors to the kitchens and finally walked into the main ballroom with all the other guests. My guards checked every room before I entered it, looking in places I never would have thought any assassin could hide. This had become routine behavior for some years now, as I was the only heir to my father's throne. Their precautions usually seemed unnecessary, but tonight I felt that perhaps they weren't being careful enough.

The lights in the main ballroom were already set up to give the room a spectrum of colors in different places, the floors were swept clean, drapes of all colors hung from the rafters, and some guests were already dancing to the lighthearted music. Mother sat on her throne, cooling herself with her favorite peacock fan (a present from a foreign prince in the Emerald Isles, she told me every time she used it).

I could see a line of young women forming in what was designated as the "dance with the king, hope he falls in love with you and makes you queen" area. I could tell, by the way they all simultaneously squealed upon noticing me, that tonight was going to be a long night. The older nobility crowded around the refreshment tables where goblets were filled to the brim with champagne and, for the older men, brandy or something else that smelled horrible. I was thinking of getting some refreshment for myself when I saw him again, that strange man.

Again, there was nothing necessarily eye-catching about him. I'd noticed him only because part of me was searching for him in the growing crowd.

He stared directly at me, something that silenced my thoughts. I was accustomed to being watched but not so directly. Sidelong glances were common, or coy little "come hither" looks from behind fans and masks. But this man just stared at me with his strange, gray eyes. He still wore his skeleton mask so I had no idea what he looked like underneath. When he noticed me staring back at him, he flashed a grin with teeth so white that I almost mistook him for a true skeleton.

The dancers parted like puppets as he walked boldly towards me, his eyes never straying from mine. I thought to run, perhaps to step back and hide behind my guards. My senses attempted to warn me that something was wrong but I couldn't move; I simply stared at him. He stopped so close that my guards moved forward threateningly.

He was shorter than I by several good inches. I could see now that his hair wasn't entirely black, but instead black with dark red highlights. This gave him the appearance of having dried blood tangled between the locks of his hair, a morbid thought for the occasion.

"A rose for you, Prince?" he said softly, his voice no higher than a husky whisper. He held out a dead black rose between his thumb and middle finger.

"Ah, thank you," I said politely, keeping my hands at my sides.

"You don't like roses, Prince," he asked, coming closer. He was too close. His presence crowded me. I scowled at the trapped feeling, instead focusing on his annoying insistence on calling me "prince." I was no longer a prince, I was King now. I also didn't like the way he said it, as if it was his own personal joke.

"I don't mind them," I said, carefully picking my words. "Why don't you give your rose to a nice young lady? There are plenty of suitable alternatives to me, who would appreciate the sentiment more than I would."

"I only want to give you this particular rose," he insisted.

"I hope you won't ask me to dance next," I said under my breath, rolling my eyes. He edged closer, a strange look on his face. Before I could protest, he'd forced the thorny weed into my hand.

"Perhaps I will, Prince," he said. He stepped back and walked away without glancing again at me. I stared after him, looking down at the rose in my hand. I wrinkled my nose and handed it over to one of my guards, wiping my hand casually on the back of my pants. The feel of it made my skin crawl, as had the man who had given it to me.

"What do you want me to do with this?" the guard whispered to me. He held it carefully, keeping the thorns well away from his skin.

"I have no idea... throw it away the first chance you get," I said. I shuddered to repel the disgusted feeling I'd gotten holding the rose and turned my thoughts to other matters.

"Christopher, come here," Mother gushed from her throne, waving for me to join her. She wore a toothy smile on her face that hid her perpetual annoyance with the world. She might have been insulted by my taste of clothes (black was never very festive, even under these circumstances) but her face didn't appear to be watching my costume nor the sluggish way I dragged my feet. She didn't drop that hideous smile either.

"Hello, Mother," I said as pleasantly as I could manage.

"Are you enjoying yourself?" she asked, placing two kisses on each of my cheeks before sitting on her velvet throne. The gold of her gown contrasted nicely with the red of her cushions, an effect I'm sure she had planned in advance.

"Now Mother, must we continue with the pleasantries? You know no one is listening to us here," I said, allowing a bit of an edge to line my words. Now that I was on my throne and looking around, I could see how color-coordinated everything was. It disgusted me how much time had gone into creating this stupid effect on the room and the guests. I especially hated how everyone seemed to be laughing.

"Be quiet and smile, Christopher," she said, still smiling. "You don't have to be such a stick in the mud. Everyone else is having a good time; why can't you?" She turned to watch the various assembled groups converse and dance. I rested, mentally drawing back. I have to find a way out of this party soon or else I'll lose my mind, I thought. I contented myself thinking of the other party that the servants would have later. Now those were good parties. They'd know how to take my mind off my father's death. I knew they actually cared that he was dead.

"Your Majesty," a soft, deep voice drew my attention back to the present. I glanced at the four bowed heads and immediately brightened, sitting closer to the edge of my seat. "We offer our condolences on this very sad day," the voice continued.

"And we also thought you could use some cheering up," a young man behind the first said with a mischievous grin. I waved at them impatiently to straighten and grinned wider, happy for the first time in days. Nikko Rannoch, the head of the Rannoch family, and his son Richard relaxed when they saw my easy grin.

"We hope that your night might brighten with our assistance, Your Majesty," the soft voice of Frederica Rannoch, the young daughter of Nikko and Amelia Rannoch, said as she gracefully bowed her head again. Richard rolled his eyes at me while his sister scraped about. I hid a smirk behind my hand so I wouldn't hurt her feelings as she knelt by my feet and looked up at me through her lashes. I noted with some interest that she'd grown into more of a woman than I had expected and she intended for me to notice the change, as she had chosen a low-cut black gown with silver designs specifically over a particular part of her anatomy.

"If there is anything we, the Rannoch family, can do for you, Your Majesty, you need only ask," Frederica continued coyly. I smiled faintly and made some assent, trying to get her to stand again. I could already see the hawk eyes of every mother in the room calculating how best to get Frederica out of the way for their own daughters while simultaneously deciding how interested I might possibly be in this new rival. Knowing what these women were thinking, I decided to hold off the bloodshed until after dinner.

"I will most assuredly inform you of any service you can perform for me, Frederica," I said. "For now, I hope you can simply enjoy the festivities. Mother has gone to great pains to accommodate our many guests." Mother smiled at me, clearly pleased that I'd noticed.

Frederica nodded solemnly, as if I'd said something particularly complex and deep, then offered me her gloved hand and looked up at me through her lashes. Wow, but she had perfected the art. I took the hand and pecked it quickly, feeling embarrassed when I saw Richard snickering at me from behind his father's back. Lady Amelia Rannoch, Nikko's lovely foreign wife, bowed as well but didn't approach me. The way she'd worn a conservative dress and done her hair in a particularly unflattering way, I knew she'd gone to great lengths to make herself unnoticeable. She wanted all the glory for her daughter.

"Frederica, my dear, you have grown so. Come here so I can see you properly. Have you bought a new corset just for this party? Do tell me where you purchased such a lovely addition to your costume," Mother said. I knew immediately that the poor girl was doomed. She'd never get away from my mother's prying eyes and barbed questions, and she'd probably never get a chance to catch me once I'd made my escape. I took the opportunity and stood, quickly sidestepping Frederica and grabbing Richard in a hug.

"When did you get back? You didn't tell me you were going to be here!" I said as I stepped back, grinning at him. He was sunburned and full of freckles, grinning. He'd worn black, as I had, and put a navy blue cloak over his shoulders to comply with the no-black rule. He looked comfortable in his clothes, whereas I was squirming to get out of mine.

"Father thought I could surprise you," Richard said as he punched me in the arm. "This party's a bit much, don't you think? I thought I'd have enough of these fancy parties after I left the Southern Lands. You have no idea how much people love to throw parties there! It's enough to make you want to run out of the room screaming. Please tell me the servants are having a decent party downstairs."

"Of course they are," I said, trying to stop grinning. Richard and I had been best friends for years and he'd been away for a long time. Our families had been strongly linked for centuries and it only made sense that we would grow up together. We'd had many an adventure that nearly got one of us killed, only bringing us closer together as friends. Getting drunk seemed like the best way to commemorate his coming home.

"Besides," Richard said, lowering his voice. "We know your dad would have much preferred anything but this. I heard some harpies by the refreshment booth saying they loved how dashing you looked in black clothes. They said you should be in mourning more often if you'd look that good all the time." We both rolled our eyes. We'd been getting this kind of reaction from girls for years. "Don't worry though, I immediately set them to rights. I told them how you were only covering up a very nasty rash," he said with a mischievous smirk.

"Gee, thanks," I said, rolling my eyes again.

"Glad to be of service, Oh Mighty One," Richard said. We'd almost succeeded in sneaking away from our families, hoping to get to the servants' party early, when we were interrupted by loud murmuring in the crowd.

The trumpeting of the announcers signaled for the crowd to quiet. By now the ballroom was full of highborn nobility and some kings and queens from neighboring countries, along with some of the rich lesser born families in the area. This had been the party to get invited to, since so many well-known people would be attending. I recognized most of them, but some seemed to be more party-crashers than invited guests.

Mother perked up in her seat, leaning forward eagerly. An announcer dressed in the castle's livery stepped onto the highest step on the grand staircase and cleared his throat. The whispers died down and everyone looked up at him, some shushing their companions. "Presenting, for the entertainment of my lords and ladies, the gravest of us here, although perhaps not so grave as our dearly departed king," this earned a chuckle, "He is the most sought-after performer in all the land, the Whisper from the Grave, the Angel of Death, the Skull Juggler!"

The crowd scattered into intrigued applause as that man, the man who had given me the rose, stepped onto the wooden platform built like a stage. Someone had thought it would be funny to hang a noose from one of the candelabra and everyone laughed upon noticing it. The Skull Juggler, intent on whatever he had planned, ignored the crowd and opened a black velvet bag by his feet. He carefully lifted five white skulls from within, some with strange markings and designs etched into them, others perfectly clean and white. He looked even more sinister now with his skull mask grinning back at the crowd. He looked down at me and I watched, transfixed, as he winked at me and threw the skulls into the air. They instantly spouted fire.

I jumped, as did everyone else in the room. Hushed whispers and excited squeals preceded a hasty applause. Richard murmured excitedly, contemplating how the Skull Juggler made the fire come out of the skulls. I half-heard it, too absorbed in the act. The man juggled the skulls as if they weighed nothing, unaffected by the crowd's reaction or the multi-colored flames. He was completely absorbed in his task just as we were absorbed by his performance.

My mouth hung wide open the entire time that I watched, my fingers clenching when he almost set his hand aflame. He remained poised and in control during all of his tricks. At one point, he tossed a flaming skull into the crowd and a woman shrieked when it exploded into a cloud of ash. The remnants fell to her feet harmlessly. Her companions cackled at her fright, although the woman didn't seem to find the situation humorous. As transfixed as I felt, a distant part of my mind felt a growing sense of dread.

He juggled more and more skulls, all of which seemed to materialize out of thin air, all the while becoming more complex and daring. The crowd howled and applauded, their eyes obsessively following his every move.

Eventually, the skulls started vanishing as seamlessly as they had appeared. When the Skull Juggler only had three remaining skulls, the crowd hushed. The finale was coming up, everyone could sense it, and everyone anticipated something amazing. I glanced away for a moment and noticed something strange.

Some members of the audience held black roses identical to the one the Skull Juggler had given me. I glanced back briefly to find my guard holding the rose limply, his eyes fastened on the performance. He shouldn't have been doing that. He should have been looking around to make sure no one would exploit this opportunity and kill me. It didn't matter, he was as transfixed as everyone else. Seemingly without thought, he lifted the rose to his face and smelled it as if the scent were something unexpected and beautiful.

All of those in the crowd with a rose smelled their own prizes excitedly, murmuring to their friends about their good fortune. Mother whispered how upset she was that she hadn't received a rose but she continued to smile to hide her irritation. Frederica quickly murmured that she would personally speak with the Skull Juggler and request a rose specifically for her. Richard was too absorbed to say anything.

"A brilliant performance," Mother cried over the crowd as they applauded. The Skull Juggler bowed as the last skull vanished. Mother laughed and stood as she applauded. There was a ripple of noise and excited murmuring from the crowd.

"Thank you, Your Majesty," he said. He bowed again as the crowd whistled and clapped.

"But where is your grand finale?" Mother asked over

the noise. I didn't think anyone could hear her over the cheering.

The Skull Juggler tilted his head, throwing shadows over his skull mask so that the white, white teeth appeared to be grinning. He bowed low, his cloak sweeping the floor.

"This, madam, is my finale," he said. A sudden burst of sound erupted from under the stage. The ground shook and then settled as the Skull Juggler vanished in a cloud of smoke. The audience began to yell and cheer louder, whooping with excitement. That was the exact moment when every single person holding a black rose fell to the floor, dead. My guard, to whom I had given the rose, was one of them.

There was silence at first. The guests hadn't realized what had happened. Then there was the first scream. In the chaos that followed, I couldn't help wondering if the Skull Juggler had done this on purpose to honor my father's death.

Interlude
The Death Festivities

Charnel, the God of Death, was a quiet and dark being who occasionally enjoyed masquerading as a mortal human to escape his morbid duties. He especially enjoyed mysterious visits to humans when there was a feast or celebration underway.

Eventually, the Dark God realized that every deity save for himself had a holy day with festivities and celebrations every single year. Even the God of War held celebrations before a great battle. Some gods had more than one celebration a year, such as during the different times of the harvest or during particularly important events. And yet there was not even a sacrificial offering for the God of Death, the god that kept the world spinning.

So, in order to remedy this offense to his great ego, Charnel appealed to the Great Mother. When she and the other gods decided against holding any kind of celebration after a death, Charnel grew furious and vengeful. He vowed to discontinue his duties until his request was granted. His twin brother Sol, the God of Life, understood the consequences. He begged the gods to reconsider but to no avail.

Perhaps if there had not been ongoing war at the time, the results would not have been so instantaneous. Soldiers refused to die during the battles or from the diseases that infected their open wounds. Instead, they lived in anguish while their comrades attempted to kill them, or while their enemies endlessly tortured them for information. Those animals used for food would not die and famines followed. Those animals cooked alive would not allow their eaters any peace until every mouthful was devoured, and even then the animals screamed from within.

Worst of all, the gods received no sacrifices. This was the most terrifying problem of all, for the gods always required sacrifices in honor of their great majesty and grace.

Within ten days, the gods ordered the death festivities to begin.

- 2 -

The Funeral

Mother quickly silenced all public talk of the Skull Juggler's performance. The funerals for each victim were held quietly and without accompanying festivities, as most people feared that such a party would only recall the Skull Juggler. All who were caught gossiping about the event were punished with a hefty fine and severe intimidation. Even I wasn't allowed to talk about it, although I did whenever I was away from anyone who could tattle on me. The servants in the castle adored me and knew that I wouldn't say anything that would get them into trouble, so they had no problem passing on the gossip to me about what others were saying. I in turn passed on the information to the librarians who documented the daily activities of the royal family.

Despite the punishments, word spread like wildfire that a true Death-waker had entered the castle and murdered thirteen people, all under the nose of the Queen and her heir, the new King. There was even a rumor that the King himself (that's me) was nearly killed as well (which was true). There were also rumors that the Skull Juggler had tortured all the other guests, who were lucky to have escaped him unscathed (which was not true). The rumor that the Skull Juggler had tortured the other guests was tame compared to some of the other rumors that circulated at the time, rumors that were further fueled by the wild imaginations of the foreign guests.

All of the guests were terrified to leave their room, or even to pass by that particular part of the castle. They walked sideways like crabs in order to keep one eye behind them and one in front, spending a great deal of money to have personal bodyguards around them at all times. Some became suspicious of their own servants, punishing them brutally in some cases and in others simply sending them away. The most terrified ones decided to kill themselves before the Skull Juggler could come back and do it for them. There were more deaths and injuries after the Skull Juggler left than there were during the death festivities.

When people panic in this way, it puts your own fears into perspective. I knew better than to fear for my life the way some of the other nobles did. Panicking would only get me hurt, so I concentrated on other matters to keep calm.

Unfortunately, I couldn't watch the terrified nobles skirt dark corners and scream every time someone came up behind them for long. Almost immediately after the Skull Juggler's performance, my best friend Richard Rannoch was sent back to the Southern Lands. He could only attend the funerals of the deceased before he left, all in the interest of keeping him out of harm's way. Nikko Rannoch also made plans to send his wife and daughter to extended family.

I can still remember the private funeral the servants held for my guard's family. I felt guilty because I couldn't remember my guard's name on the day of his funeral, and I was too embarrassed to ask his family, especially when I found out that he was related to some of the servants I knew personally. As King, I wasn't supposed to know any of the kitchen staff. Because I don't like to do what I'm supposed to, these became people I thought of as close friends.

Although I wasn't supposed to know any of the servants, I was expected to know my guards. At the first least, I needed to know their names – or at least, it was expected of me, especially because I saw most of them for hours on end. The deceased's family had this same expectation and kept asking me what I'd thought of the guard and if he'd been a good protector for me. I couldn't handle the shame for long and, right after his last rites were spoken over his coffin, I escaped from the group of mourners and went to see Richard.

He'd gone to huddle beside a group of faded marble gravestones, hissing into his hands to bring them warmth. Although he'd technically been born in Roc, he should have been accustomed to the cold long ago. Because of his extensive travels to lands far south of Roc, however, he'd grown accustomed to warmer climates instead. I would have teased him about it, except that I was annoyed about my current problems.

I'd asked him how long he would stay in Roc, now that this whole mess had happened. I had little hope of him staying in the country, what with such a grave threat to his life. As the only male heir to his family's land and property, his life had to be guarded in the same way that mine was. After the death of my old guard, a new one now stayed a claustrophobic five feet away as we conversed, his expression blank. The biting-cold wind didn't seem to bother him either.

Richard was in the middle of grumbling about his paranoid father and needing to leave as soon as possible. It was a conversation we'd had ever since he was six years old and leaving for a boarding school far away.

"If it was up to me," Richard said bitterly, "I'd stick around and see what happens. Dad said there were some signs of trouble close to home and that he was certain we'd see some sort of political or social action in at least a year or two. He said it would just be a matter of time before someone tried to use the Skull Juggler's show to get ahead somehow. And naturally I don't get to see any of it happen."

"Gee, thanks for worrying about my life," I said, grinning. "You do realize that whatever trouble your dad was talking about will probably affect me directly, right? I could be killed for all you know."

Richard snorted and bounced on the balls of his feet, smirking at me. "Not that it would be a waste to humanity if you did," he said. "I think he's just worrying for nothing. He's even sending Frederica away. Mom is getting on his case over it. She's obsessed with getting Frederica married to you." He rolled his eyes as he said this. I shuddered and leaned against one of the headstones, resting my temple against the freezing stone without feeling too bothered by it. I didn't have Richard's problem with cold weather.

"Thank your dad for me whenever you get the chance. I for one am happy to get a break from her. I've known your sister for years and, at the same time, know absolutely nothing about her except that she's very clearly obsessed with me," I said. Richard snorted and pulled his cloak more tightly around his arms. We watched as a group of women from one of the other funerals passed us, one of them crying softly into her hand as she pulled a small child down the hill. The child stared at us, his eyes very wide. Richard cursed softly and leaned back, staring up at the sky.

"As much as I'd like to see what happens next, I'm a little glad I'm leaving," he said.

"Oh?" I said, still watching the woman with her child. The bottom of her black dress was stained with mud and grass. She didn't seem to care all that much about how she looked. "Don't tell me you're getting paranoid too."

"It's not being paranoid," Richard said. "The Skull Juggler, whoever the hell he is… he killed people. He killed a lot of people, in plain view of highly trained soldiers and a whole lot of witnesses who could do nothing about him. No one knows who or what he is, where he is, what he wants. That sort of adversary is lethal. How can you anticipate his next move if you have no idea what he's capable of?"

I tore my eyes from the woman's back and glanced at him. Richard's face appeared relaxed at that moment, but I could see the tension in his hands. He was really worried about this.

"You aren't worried about me, are you?" I asked. He

glanced at me and then quickly away, shrugging nonchalantly.

"It'd be a pity if you died. You're the only person I know who willingly puts up with me," he said. I frowned, surprised he was worried enough to think I was somehow in danger.

"Richard..." I said, unsure how to speak my thoughts, "I live in the highest tower of a castle, a fortress actually, surrounded by guards at all times, day and night, without interruption. I have both magical and physical protection from any surprise attacks, a strong network of spies who are constantly on the lookout for conspiracies against my life, a group of loyal servants who watch for intruders at all times, and I'm not stupid. I'll be fine."

"I know," Richard said as he grinned at me. He still looked worried but I didn't push him, shrugging.

"Just saying, you shouldn't worry about what will happen to me. I'm probably going to be the bored one. You know what'll happen – Mother will lock me away from the world, the servants will check my food and taste it first to make sure there aren't any poisons in it, I won't be able to fart without someone rushing in thinking the worst." Richard snickered so I grinned and kept going. "Meanwhile you'll be traveling through the Southern Lands to the university again and you'll get to meet all kinds of interesting people. You'll have all your fun with the beautiful girls and brag about knowing a very powerful and exotic king in the north."

Richard rolled his eyes. "It's not all about you, you know. I get plenty of action without needing to drudge your name up during conversation. I think all this cold air is going to your head," he said.

"It's what I've been saying all along," I said. "Mother will lock me in my room and I'll go even more insane. Just watch... if the Skull Juggler doesn't kill me, being cooped up all day will."

It had been a good conversation and after we'd gotten the serious talk out of the way, we moved on to other subjects. He swore to write to me about all the gorgeous women in the Southern Lands, as well as the legendary bazaars with merchants from all over the world, and he swore he would invite me to visit with him as soon as he could. I swore in turn to write back about how bored I was with the occasional reference to the servants' parties and any other interesting rumors going around about the Skull Juggler and political uprisings.

When his father came looking for him, we parted after exchanging pleasantries. Nikko told me to expect some communication with him soon and left with Richard in tow, both looking identically glum. I returned to the castle with my bodyguard, both content and saddened by the departure of my friend. Richard left Roc soon after our conversation.

Upon noting Nikko Rannoch's behavior with his wife and children, Mother became adamant about my safety and did everything in her power to keep me occupied, or perhaps she wanted me out of the way while she calmed a potential uprising. She did exactly what I suspected she would do – she locked me up in the castle. The library became my only refuge as she worked diligently to dose the fires such an invasion of safety the recent deaths provided. Mathew, my advisor, gave me the watered-down version of the happenings in the castle while Armand spoke more bluntly of the problems in the kingdom.

The Skull Juggler danger was real, paranoia or not. The Kingdom of Roc was infamous for having built its city on the graves of an ancient people. According to the myth, the graves belonged to betrayed warriors, a people who had been destroyed by the same God they had worshipped for eons. A Death-waker, as the Skull Juggler's type of magician was called, could potentially raise this threat. It was for this reason that if even the rumor of such a man was heard, the current monarch was blamed and hanged. Mother, far more aware of this danger than anyone else, understood the need to calm everyone down and therefore did everything she could to soothe the fears running rampant.

She went out among the people during even the smallest parades, lowered taxes throughout the kingdom, offered shelter to the homeless, and generally made herself a prominent, helpful person everywhere she could. She offered all sorts of personal favors to the upper classes as well, something that annoyed me until Armand explained that this was one of the smartest moves she'd made so far. With their support, she had more a better chance of protecting herself if anything happened in the castle. Following the same logic, she gave the servants more free days, increased their wages, and helped their family members enter the service of the castle for exceptional benefits. This strengthened the servants' loyalty to us, especially to her. She also tightened the security within the castle itself so that only those that were specifically invited to the castle could enter. There were some small misunderstandings where the local boyfriends of some of the younger maids were captured and incarcerated until the maids admitted to knowing the men. Social visits were, after this particular event, suspended for the servants.

As for me, this meant more hours of solitude in my chambers or in the library. Why isolation was the best course of action, I'll never know. I could, for example, have been doing public relations work with my people and learning how to deal with a political crisis. The point was to distract the public, I soon realized. To distract the people would help life return to normal.

Distractions, however, couldn't get in the way of necessary celebrations. One such event was the birthday of my cousin, who had been promised an outrageously overpriced coming-of-age birthday party in the castle, ever since she was old enough to understand what a birthday party was.

It was a particularly cold morning on the day of my cousin's birthday, which meant that I was comfortably cocooned in my warm sheets with pillows on top of my head for more darkness. The drapes to my bed were drawn despite the added curtains on my windows (which faced the east so that the sun could blind me every time I forgot to close them) and I was blissfully unaware of the world outside of my sanctuary. I'd roused a little at a sound somewhere in my room but I began to doze off again, thinking my guards would protect me from whatever mouse had nibbled through the plaster, when someone cleared his throat from behind the drapes.

That someone pulled said drapes open, loudly,

rudely, and sunlight speared my eyes and all over me. I hissed like a cat drenched in water and shielded my eyes, absurdly awake. The man cleared his throat, more apologetically this time, and stood in front of the sun's rays. I could see now that he wore the castle's livery and held his hat under his arm. He looked at me as if preparing for a great battle and sucked in his stomach. Pieces of his face, his delicate nose, the chipmunk-like cheeks, his small watery eyes, came together in a memory and I realized who this must be.

"Her Majesty wishes an audience with you, Your Majesty," Stewart, my mother's porter, said with a graceful bow. This action alone was partly restricted by his generous belly and the tight material of his waistcoat. I sat up, hair ruffled and in various directions, eyes bloodshot and glaring at this intrusion on my sanity. I promptly threw a pillow at the man and turned over, prepared to ignore him for the rest of the morning.

"Your Majesty, please," Stewart said. He had already guessed my plan and moved to interrupt it before I fell back asleep. "Your lady cousin will be having her birthday party this evening," he said earnestly. His earnestness was annoying. I wanted to throw another pillow at him but it was treacherously located under my head. What had he said? Party? Was he trying to make me think at this ungodly hour? What time was it anyway?

I grew annoyed with myself, realizing I was unleashing my frustrations on this man, who'd only ever done what he was ordered to do for the entire time I'd known him. The person I was really angry with was Mother. It wasn't his fault that my family was utterly horrible and chose the worst times to have parties. It wasn't Stewart's fault that he had to wake me in the morning when I was the most irritable and muddled. I contemplated lengthy and creative tortures for Mother as I collected what little patience I had.

"Whose birthday is it again," I grumbled as I swung my legs over the edge of the bed, resisting the urge to chuck another pillow at something, anything, just to get my frustration out. He bowed again, deeper this time (though I don't know how he managed to do this).

"Lady Evelyn is turning fifteen, I am told," he said soothingly. Ah, I'd forgotten which of my many cousins was supposed to be here. After all the time I'd spent isolated in my room, I felt fairly disconnected from the outside world. Evelyn... of course I remembered Evelyn. If I could just wake up a little, I'd be more specific about what I remembered. As the name registered in the back of my mind, I remembered bits and pieces of my interactions with Evelyn, more specifically my relationship with her parents.

I hated Evelyn's parents, related through my father's side, with a burning passion. Knowing them as I did, they were sure to be around. Evelyn, I remembered, had been interesting when we'd been growing up together. She'd become a shy, annoyingly sweet young woman as she matured, probably through the influence of her mother. Her kind disposition made associating with her difficult, especially when she came with her parents trailing not-too-far behind. Evelyn's parents, like Amelia Rannoch, had been competing for years to make their daughter the most attractive person in the world to me. This meant that they'd taught her to always be polite, lady-like, and submissive to me at all times. I really didn't want to deal with her particular brand of submissiveness this early in the morning. She always agreed with everything I said and right now, I really wanted to argue with someone.

"Oh, is she? And why does Mother want me to get up now? I assume she wants her birthday bash in the evening like all the other girls her age?" I ran a hand over my eyes, trying to become politer. It really wasn't fair the way I was acting like a spoiled jerk. "What is it that I'm meant to do right now?"

"Her Majesty would prefer that you join her and your cousin's family for breakfast. She has arrangements that she wishes to discuss with you, Your Majesty," Stewart said. He wouldn't look at me as he spoke, constantly glancing sidelong at the door, the window, the drapes, anything but me. I frowned and slumped out of bed, walking towards the windows. As I passed him, I noticed the sweat standing out starkly against his pale forehead. He still refused to meet my eyes, even after I handed him a handkerchief to dry his face.

"There's more to this than what you're telling me," I said at last. He jerked back, eyes wide. This only confirmed my guess. "Why does she want me to go to breakfast with her? Who else is going to be there? Why is it important that I get up now instead of later for Evelyn's birthday?" Stewart gnawed on his bottom lip, shuffling his feet.

"Your Majesty, please. I cannot talk about it. It is only gossip after all, just the maids overhearing tidbits of information and thinking themselves clever for figuring out what will happen! Please Your Majesty, don't make me tell you! It's really not true, Sire, please!" I arched an eyebrow. Something about his face told me he was dying to tell me whatever he was withholding. Yes, he wanted me to beg him.

"What is it?" I finally sighed, rubbing my temples. Too early for this, far too early to deal with this, I thought.

"S-Since you compel me, Your Majesty, I shall tell you," he said. He took a deep breath, leaning closer to me. "Sire, it has been said that the Queen was discussing matters with your aunt and uncle. There was gossip about a huge party and... a dowry." He leaned towards me, his face eager for my reaction. I stared at him blankly.

"A dowry?" I repeated without much interest. "She's getting married, is she? I feel sorry for the stupid bloke who ends up having to spend the rest of his life with her family." Stewart continued staring at me in a funny way. I stared back at him for a long time before realization hit me. I groaned, turned around, and flopped back into bed and pulled the covers over my head.

"Your Majesty?" Stewart whimpered.

"Go away," I hissed from underneath. No, I wasn't going to even think about it. I wasn't even going to contemplate what that could mean. Stewart hesitated, probably calculating how angry I would be, and then came to poke me through the sheets.

"Your Majesty, please," he said nervously, "you must get up."

"I'm not going to marry Evelyn," I informed him calmly. "I'd rather marry my horse."

It wasn't that Evelyn was evil, or even that she was

an annoying brat anymore. She was certainly younger than I was, but Mother had been the same age when she'd married my father. Evelyn didn't talk annoyingly for hours and hours and she didn't spend exuberant amounts of other men's money (unlike Frederica Rannoch). She wasn't known for being a loose woman, she had never been deflowered (as my mother delicately put it), and she didn't have any eligible bachelors waiting for her in the wings that I knew of. She was calm, quiet, sweet, generous, and boring. I had nothing against those characteristics, I really didn't, but I did not want to marry Evelyn. I didn't want to marry anyone. I groaned again as the poking continued.

"Please, Your Majesty, get up," Stewart pleaded. "Lord Mathew said that you must go at once or he shall be very cross with me. Please, Sire, you must get up." He sounded near tears. I groaned louder this time and removed the covers, glaring up at him.

"Fine, I'm getting up. But I'm not marrying her," I said.

"Of course not, Your Majesty," he said soothingly. Feeling heavier and older, I dragged myself out of bed, still glaring at him. I nearly expected him to burst out laughing and say "Ha! You have to marry into your uncle's family!" He didn't, of course, and it was stupid of me just to imagine it. But I did anyway.

Interlude
The First Necromancer

The first Necromancer walked the land Alone. He saw Death everywhere he traveled, feeling the pull of his own nature, demanding he maintain the balance of life and death. He did not question his lot in life, nor did he mind his work, but he was miserable for many years.

One day, he realized why he was so terribly unhappy. He was afraid that he would enjoy harming those around him. He was afraid that he would be driven insane and kill and kill and kill and soon, there would be none but him left. He was afraid that he would be left Alone forever.

The God of Death came at his bidding.

"What is it you desire?" the God of Death asked.

"I wish for a companion. I do not want to be Alone forever. I do not want to kill everyone. I do not want to be driven insane by this need."

And the Death God remembered His own Loneliness and Isolation from all other Gods and how He often wished such a barrier did not exist between Himself and His brothers and sisters.

And so He granted His first Necromancer the ability to create more Necromancers, but only under very specific circumstances and only after he had picked the ones he wanted. He did this so that his work could be done more quickly, for despite the power of the First Necromancer, there was much work to be done and less and less time to do it in. The God of Death did all of this, secretly, out of Pity.

- 3 -
THE DEAL

I put on my usual clothes (black for mourning Father) and a warm cloak around my shoulders since it was cold in the castle. Feeling increasingly more childish, I made my way down to the kitchen, making sure to shuffle my feet to make Mother wait. Stewart only followed me a few steps before my guards pointedly stopped him. They looked more tense than usual, I noted distantly, and they very quickly directed Stewart in another direction. He wisely retreated to whichever hole he'd crawled out of. It was a relief to be alone again and be as angry as I wanted to be, as my guards did not gossip about me to anyone.

As I went through the main study on the ground floor towards the private dinning room where my guests undoubtedly waited for me, I instead switched direction and went to the kitchen. When I saw the familiar jolly faces of the cooks laughing and joking with each other, making sexual jokes and relatively having a wonderful time, I felt myself relax. This was exactly what I needed before facing Mother and my other guests. I couldn't let them see how furious I was at being roused from bed so early.

"Here comes the King," one of them gushed when she noticed me standing by the door.

"What in the world are you doing out of bed so early? Well, come in, dearie. We can't feed you if you're standing out there," Maggie Milkins said. She gathered me into a bear hug, all the while patting me in inappropriate places as she ushered me inside. They bustled around the stoves and catcalled louder for my benefit. I grinned and pretended to be embarrassed by their creative innuendos, though they knew better than to feel ashamed of treating me like, well, a little prince.

"Now, to what do we owe this great honor," Abigail Baker asked at me. She was one of the younger girls, thirteen or so. She had grown up with me sneaking into the kitchens and stealing all the sweets I was forced to abstain from in the presence of high-browed guests. She was also very good at poking me with a wooden spoon when she caught me dipping my fingers into the cake batters and stealing cream before breakfast.

"You never come visit us anymore," she said, adopting the sensuous tone of voice the older serving girls used whenever they saw me. With her, the effect was comical. "I'm starting to think you've fallen in love with someone else," she said.

"I could never love any so much as you, my darling Abigail," I said, flicking the end of her frizzy pigtails. Maggie laughed at my very serious declaration of love and affection, poking me with her spoon, greatly reminding me of how Mother treated her royal scepter. No one ever seemed to believe me when I told them I was deeply in love with them, like in that Cinderella story I'd read a long time ago. I insisted often (and loudly) that I was determined that one of them was secretly a princess and that the second I found a decent shoemaker, you could bet I would have a magnificent ball to which they were all cordially invited. Abigail and Maggie especially liked to laugh at me over this.

"Honestly, you haven't been around here for a while," Abigail said, her playful tone melting into concern. "We weren't sure they'd ever let you out again after all the... all the gossip going around about that night." A collective hush filled the kitchen as every person strained to hear my response.

"I've been locked in a tower," I said in as serious a tone of voice as I could muster, "waiting for my princess to arrive and rescue me. They promised me all kinds of things... a kiss, marriage, a whole lot of money..." the servants started jeering and booing at me, throwing various rags. I laughed and covered my head with my hands. Abigail turned a pretty shade of red, making her frizzy blonde hair and green eyes light up. I felt something strange, looking at her blushing like that.

"You're so cute," I said impulsively. The loud cheers surprised me, as I'd forgotten I had an audience. Abigail turned an even brighter shade of red as she stared at me, her eyes a little wide. I think she knew I was serious.

"Aye, when are the two of you tying the knot?" one of the other women said with a laugh.

"The knot to his noose, no doubt," one whispered to another, who giggled. Abigail whipped her spoon at them. The spoon flung bits of sauce at them, sauce that would probably be part of my midday meal. The girls squealed and jumped away, shrieking with laughter.

"In all seriousness, when are you getting engaged? I've started hearing rumors..." Marianne asked in a whisper. She waved away some of the more daring serving girls with her frying pan. They peeked at me over her shoulder anyway, giggling when they caught my attention.

"Some time in the spring, I expect," I said gravely, "though I much prefer the winter since I'll have something warm to look forward to at night." I winked at the women as they laughed harder, chiding and poking each other.

Abigail blushed and scowled darkly at me, her shoulders trembling. Part of me felt bad for making the joke, as it seemed to hurt her feelings that I had been honest before and callous now. I felt even more embarrassed about the slip I'd just made, saying that she was cute. She was, of course, too young for me and more of a little sister than a love interest. I had the sneaking suspicion that she actually did have a crush on me, despite how playfully she behaved around the other cooks.

We were just getting into a very good conversation about a party some of the local bakers were having outside of the castle and who would be going when I heard that voice again.

"Excuse me, Sire," I closed my eyes and groaned. There, Stewart again. And I'd thought I'd lost him. "I'm sorry to disturb you, Sire, but the Queen has asked me to remind you of the time. Your guests are awaiting your arrival."

"With abated breath, no doubt," I stood reluctantly.

"You're leaving already?" Maggie grunted. "So like

you, little brat. Get out of our sight before I send your jealous lovers after you." I mock gasped and hurried out of the kitchen, although this was the last thing I wanted to do. What I would have done to stay there and bask in the warmth of their discussions. Even having Abigail mad at me was better than facing people right then. Taking a deep breath and plastering a pleasant, charming smile on my face, I took the corridor from the kitchen to the private dinning room.

The ten foot mahogany table practically groaned under the sparkling porcelain dishes and silverware, piled to bursting with all manner of foods. I took a quick surveillance of the room out of habit, something my guards had been teaching me to do, and noticed where every person in the room was. Mother sat in her normal spot at the end of the table. She was raised up slightly so that she could see over the mountain of food and I could see from her plate that she hadn't touched anything in front of her. She whispered to one of the servants, who bowed before he left the room, and then looked up at me. Something about her expression made me pause. She looked nervous, something she never showed in front of company. I frowned and kept looking around.

I noticed that there were three unfamiliar guards standing behind three chairs, all men that I distantly recognized from various parties and events. My aunt, uncle, and cousin sat in the three chairs, smiling up at me as I came in.

"There he is," Mother cooed in a voice dripping with sickening sweetness, the nervousness nicely masked by her voice. I considered turning right around and leaving them stunned and confused, but my path was blocked by the brown-nosing Stewart. To keep from running into him, I made a bee-line for Mother.

Kissing her cheek as was customary for a fond prince to greet his queen mother, I noticed that her hand trembled when she touched my arm. I frowned down at her, a question in my eyes. She smiled a little and indicated my seat with her head. This was strange behavior from her but I knew better than to bring it up in front of these particular guests. I nodded to my relatives and moved towards the head of the table.

I paused beside my Uncle Albert's seat. He'd stolen the chair at the head of the table, a position that was strictly mine based on etiquette and social class. The obnoxious man stared blankly at me for a moment and only seemed to understand what the problem was when his wife cleared her throat nervously. He stood with great difficulty and bowed me into my rightful throne. It was lumpy now and in the shape of his rear end (which was larger than mine) so I quietly removed the seat pillow and sat on the bare wood. Stewart materialized behind me and took the pillow away behind his back. He must have worried my uncle's feelings would be hurt.

Uncle Albert didn't notice Stewart's hasty retreat but Mother certainly did. She sent me a strange look over her juice but the strained smile never once left her lips. I ignored her pointedly, punishment for having pressured me out of bed, possibly to get married to my cousin. I concentrated instead on creative ways I could get Abigail to forgive me. Perhaps finding her something nice, like an embroidered apron, would get her to forgive me. I'd heard one of the girls babbling about how much Abigail wanted one... perhaps Evelyn would know where I could find one.

Speaking of which, she sat a few seats to my left, ducking her head shyly (coyly, I reminded myself) and politely playing with her napkin. She was a pretty girl, plain by some standards. Golden locks of straight hair (someone had attempted to curl it, I could already see signs of the hours of work coming undone) and a pale blue gown that accentuated her flat chest and nonexistent curves. She looked every bit the child I remembered her to be, though she was looking at me with a woman's eyes. Interested eyes.

I felt very uncomfortable scrutinizing her and wished that I hadn't removed the seat cushion after all. I would have felt taller with it. There was a relative silence at the table as my cousin and I observed each other. Someone, a new serving girl I'd never seen before, bowed to each of us as she brought us our hard boiled eggs in a porcelain bowl. I was tempted to grab her and beg her to change places with me, but that would have been rude. Besides, I could see that the serving girl was timid, probably unaccustomed to serving directly to royalty. I wasn't that cruel, I decided, and waited for someone to start a conversation.

"So," began my uncle, playing with his napkin, "how is your health, Sire? I'd heard you had a cold some time ago. I hope Your Majesty is feeling better."

It was a strange thing, hearing my father's brother calling me by the title he had once used for someone else. He used to call me "brat" and found several excuses to have me whipped for stupid things like using his favorite horse or making fun of him with the servants. Yes, my uncle definitely loved and respected me. Right.

He liked to be in control, a sad trait considering his lack of ruling status. Even if I were to die, and my mother died, and if I had siblings and they died, there would still be other blood relatives closer to the throne than he. According to Mother, my grandfather and Uncle Albert had gotten into a nasty fight and, as a result, Albert and all of his children were banned from ascending the throne through their direct bloodline. The only way his family could rule at all was if his family married into my family (cue Evelyn). And as much as I wanted to believe the best in my uncle and trust him, I could tell he liked sitting in my seat far too much and that he thirsted for power he dared not even speak of. This sort of attitude was not conducive to my health.

"I'm as healthy as healthy can be," I said cheerfully, just to rub it in. I suppose I was a brat. "And how are you, Uncle? Well, I hope."

"Oh, very well, Sire. I have been having some bowel problems of late, but nothing I can't handle. I'm not sure what it could have been, perhaps some food disagreed with my stomach, but I'm sure it can be cleared up easily enough," he said. I nearly dropped my cup. It always unnerved me how much uncle was willing to talk about his bodily functions at the breakfast table. Mother often complained of gas while I was in the middle of chewing.

"I'm sorry to hear that," I said once I was sure I wouldn't make an inappropriate face. "Have you sent for chamomile tea? It is quite helpful, or so I have been told."

"Oh, I hadn't thought of that," he sounded sheepish. Humbled. Humbled. By my suggestion for tea. This from the same man who'd slithered out of my chair under protest. I felt the discomfort raise a notch. "You are wise beyond your years, my king." I looked at him fully now with both eyes, not sideways as I had been doing before. He shrank back a little when I did, but upon finding some inner strength, he squared his shoulders and sat straighter in his chair. "That is a useful trait in a king."

"I should hope so," Mother said. She was smothering her toast in banana jam imported from my distant relatives in the Emerald Isles. She did so love that jam… At that moment she was lathering it on her bread as if she would never have another slice without it ever again. Her hands were still shaking a little, something that gave me pause. What was she so nervous about?

"Yes, quite right," Uncle Albert said, again humble. "Such a king would rule his kingdom well, especially with a good queen by his side." Ah, I thought, here it comes. I turned my attention away and focused on my food, moving various things around to form shapes.

"All of this over a bit of advice about bowel movements," I said casually, poking at my eggs. I knew Mother wanted to step on my foot, so I pulled my toes under my chair out of habit.

"Er, yes," he said, embarrassed now. He must have realized the two thoughts didn't fit together as well as they had in his head. "What I meant to say, Sire, is that you have a profound wisdom that few others possess. And at your age, such a trait is in high demand. One can never be too careful, in these times." He looked meaningfully at me. I looked at him sideways.

"You are, of course, referring to the Skull Juggler," I said. My aunt flinched.

"Indeed I am, Sire," he said gravely, patting her hand to soothe her. "We must make the best of our lives while we still have them. We must not tarry when making important decisions." He was leaning closer to me every time he spoke. I could feel his eyes probing me.

"We mustn't become paranoid either," I said. "After all, the time we have has always been short, even before the Skull Juggler came. The death festivities held for Father are proof of just how quickly a life can be shortened. You, of course, remember that your brother is dead." I looked at him directly as I said this. He drew back and frowned at me, clearly disappointed. Mother trembled but for the life of me, I couldn't understand why. She was never this skittish around my uncle.

"Christopher..." she said in a warning, light voice, "Mind your manners while we are eating."

"I had forgotten that death makes you ill at ease, Mother. Forgive me," I said without looking at her. I went back to poking my eggs, not feeling all that hungry. I myself had brought up my father's death but it always sickened me to think about it. He had been murdered. That was not something that I accepted with grace. I had a sinking feeling my uncle may have been involved in some way, but there was no way for me to find out or prove anything.

I didn't really want to anyway. Father had always told me that he wanted to die in the heat of battle and, judging by the scene of his death, he'd put up one hell of a fight. Either way, he wouldn't have wanted me to dwell on him. Dead was dead.

"Your Majesty, you should not speak of such things when they upset you," Evelyn said. The tension dissipated the second she opened her mouth. Uncle Albert finally stopped frowning and seemed surprised she'd spoken at all. "We should discuss happier things, shouldn't we? Such matters are so depressing."

I wanted to snap at her, to say something rude and derogatory because I felt angry about the whole morning, but I couldn't. Instead, I leaned back and pushed my plate away. Mother lowered her haunches and also returned to her food, though she ate nothing. Uncle Albert, unlike Mother and I, ate with vigorous interest and cleaned his plate and two more helpings.

"You must give a speech to my birthday party. It will be tonight, you know," Evelyn said and broke the silence with a quick clap. I looked up at her in confusion. Why she thought I could somehow weasel my way out of going to a party that was in my own castle, I didn't know. She didn't seem to realize this weird coincidence either because she ignored my facial expression. "Oh, it'll be darling! Auntie was so sweet, letting me have the party here! Thank you!"

Mother gave her a thin smile. "You're welcome, Evelyn. It was my pleasure. And do not concern yourself. Christopher will attend, of course."

"I can introduce you to all of my friends," she said

excitedly. "Oh, there's Mystiza, she's from the Emerald Isles, and Katarina, and Ursula, and Raquel, and oh, they'll love you," she bounced in her seat as she spoke, laughing gleefully. I shifted uncomfortably, unsure how to handle this new and entirely too enthusiastic version of a girl who'd never even looked me in the eye before.

"I am sure he will be a wonderful companion," Mother said meaningfully. "Christopher can be more charming than he leads us to believe."

"Yes, yes," my uncle joined in again. He looked sufficiently happier since eating. "Evelyn has a number of good friends in many provinces. Most don't visit here anymore since Roc is so isolated, but they've decided to come just for Evelyn's birthday."

"They showed an especial interest in meeting my cousin," Evelyn said, cutting off her father's last word. My aunt finally came to life, trying to calm her daughter.

"Darling," Evelyn's mother said uneasily, "remember your manners." Evelyn could not be calmed once she got going, it seemed.

"Oh please, Momma. Can't you see he looks interested? Anyway, Katarina said that she's met a few princes but she never met a king before who was our age, or a little older than us. They're great fun and they've all traveled to the most exotic places you've ever heard of! They know the most scandalous gossip from all over and they have so many stories from foreign countries, you wouldn't believe them if they spoke the bare-faced truth. Please say you'll talk to them for me? Please, cousin?"

I hesitated, feeling ambushed. Here I was, hoping for a nice, quiet, torturous morning and a successful escape once the party started (it's easier to hide in a crowd than in a small group of people, I've learned) but she was trying to pull me into a promise. And I didn't break my promises, this she knew from all the dares I had been suckered into as a child.

"I'll talk to them," I said, forcing a smile. Evelyn leapt out of her chair to hug me, laughing. Her mother looked as if she was suffering from an ulcer, watching her daughter attack me and acting like a hyperactive chipmunk. I was fairly certain there was no reference page in any etiquette book for dealing with hyperactive chipmunks.

"Oh, you're such a darling!" Evelyn cooed and then she kissed me. This shocked me even more than her strange personality switch.

I had been kissed by girls before, and I liked kissing well enough, but this was Evelyn, my possible future wife, my cousin, fifteen. I must have turned to stone because Evelyn shook me a little after she had finished her happy tantrum.

"Cousin? Are you alright?" she said as she poked my shoulder.

"Fine," I said between clenched teeth. "Excuse me, I have some things I have to do." I tried to stand but Mother leaned forward, gesturing for me to sit. I looked down at her hand, expecting to see a claw pointing at me instead of her pale, long fingers.

"Nonsense, I have made sure that you can spend the whole day with Evelyn," she said, ignoring my expression as it fell to pieces. Evelyn smiled brightly, blissfully unaware of my expression either.

"Oh, can he really? That would be so darling!" she said.

"I really should be doing state work. You know, Mother, since you told me I should take a more active part in government since Father died," I insisted, feeling trapped. Gods no, please don't make me spend the day with her. Please don't make me babysit her. Please... please.

"You will spend the day with your cousin on her birthday," Mother said as she narrowed her eyes in a way that silenced argument.

"Fine," I hissed this. Standing, I nodded to my uncle and his wife as they too stood to bow to me. "I will go and change into more proper attire. Please excuse me," while I go hang myself. Evelyn beamed after me as I practically ran out of the room. I didn't even look around as I went through the secret passage back to my room, where I started yelling and throwing things.

Interlude
The Black Roses

Once, long ago, there lived a fisherman and his wife. Every day, the fisherman left his hut by the sea and every night he brought home a fish. While he was gone, his wife went to their local parish and tended to the roses in the garden. She helped them grow with her kindness and her gentle hands, nurturing them to grow beautiful and strong. The duke of this land saw these beautiful flowers and begged the priest of the parish to give them to him for his wedding, for his beautiful bride-to-be loved roses. The priest agreed, knowing that the duke had great power and could do harm to his small community if angered.

The fisherman's wife grew sad when she was told that her beautiful roses would be cut up and killed for the wedding of a stranger. One week before the wedding, she died of a broken heart by the roses. In their turn, the roses grew black and more beautiful with their woe that the fisherman's wife was dead.

The poor fisherman did not know how to grieve his wife's death. They had both been old and approaching their deaths but her death had been sudden and painful. For the next week, the fisherman rose in the morning and returned at night with a fish. After he'd eaten, he would go to the rose garden in his parish to see the flowers his good wife had tended for so long. The priest came upon the fisherman the day before the duke's wedding and saw the sad, long face of the fisherman in the moonlight.

"These roses were grown for the wedding of a great duke," the priest explained to the fisherman. "I am sorry, but we must cut all the roses tonight."

The fisherman understood and asked only for a single rose to remember his wife. The priest, taking pity on the poor man, plucked a beautiful black rose from the bush and gave it to the fisherman with the Seventh God's blessing.

The following day, the fisherman returned home with his fish. He was tired and hungry, so he did not think of the duke's wedding. He was lonely and sore, so he thought instead of his wife. The pain in his chest grew as he thought of her and remembered long ago when they had been young and in love.

Close to midnight, as the fisherman ate his fish, thinking about his once-beautiful wife, he touched the rose from the parish gardens. Death, who haunted the house ever since the fisherman's wife died, touched the fisherman's shoulder in sympathy for his pain. The fisherman choked on a fish spine and died, his fingers clenching around the black rose.

At the duke's wedding, the guests also died, for they were now surrounded by flowers of death. It is for this reason that black roses are a terrible omen at weddings.

To ward off this omen, white lilies are now customary at funerals to remind the God of Death of those who are alive and those who are dead.

- 4 -
Last Rites

My chambers are located on the East side of the castle in the tallest of all the towers. The hidden passage in the third floor library is the only direct route to my rooms but, otherwise, there were several complicated selections of catacombs that lead to my room, including a passage from the main study on the ground floor. There were other entrances to the catacombs, such as through the kitchens, the coat room (although this one could be troublesome if there are too many guests), in the cellar, and various other rooms on different floors. My rooms were specifically chosen for me because of my role as the sole heir to the throne: they had to be as difficult to get to as possible.

Another interesting little fact about my room was that my window was hidden from the outside by both enchantments and architecture. This was great for defense, but horrible for sunlight. It was also for this reason that my room was constantly drenched in light, especially in the morning when I was trying to stay asleep. It was because of this tendency for light that I didn't realize that there was someone else in my room aside from my guards.

Armand, my tailor, smiled faintly when he noticed how furious I was. I scowled and paced by my bed, trying to work off my frustrated energy, before I could face him. He was accustomed to my temper tantrums after years of dressing me and he watched me pace with a patient smile on his face.

"I won't do it," I hissed at last, glaring at him as if this was all his idea. "I won't marry her. I'd rather be locked up forever than marry her."

Armand chuckled, watching me pace. "I see that the queen finally told you," he said.

"Mother did not tell me anything," I said. "She allowed Stewart to tell me through gossip and then trapped me into spending the rest of the day with Evelyn."

"She didn't tell you herself?" Armand said, sounding surprised. "I was certain she had taken you aside this morning to tell you of her decision."

"It should not have been her decision to make!" I raged, kicking the edge of my desk. It made a very satisfactory crunching sound and hurt my foot tremendously. "I'm King now and I should be allowed to decide who I will marry, not her!"

"She didn't have a choice," Armand said with a frown. "She should have told you all of this already. Don't you know of the meeting last night?"

"Meeting?" I echoed, a glimmer of sanity dissolving my anger. "What meeting? I don't know anything about any meeting."

"The captains of the guard and your father's network of spies conferred yesterday with your mother," Armand explained. I stopped pacing and looked at him, frowning. Why hadn't I been part of this meeting? I hesitantly sat on the edge of my bed, watching him. "There were some strong rumors circulating that there would be an attempt on your life during your cousin's birthday. No one has been able to determine where this threat will come from. All we know is that you may not be safe even inside the castle."

I snorted, reclining now that I'd heard his news. This was nothing new to me. I'd been raised under a constant shadow of terror when it became clear I was the only child my father had ever planned to have. Every day, it seemed, there was yet another rumor or suspicion or hint that my life might end at any moment.

"If that's the only reason I'm supposed to marry Evelyn, I'm not impressed," I said. "I understand that people are becoming impatient for me to wed but I doubt you'll have angry mothers storming the castle any time soon." Armand arched an eyebrow and relaxed, watching me with cool eyes.

"Your uncle has offered his protection under the condition that you marry his daughter," Armand said. "He has sworn never to make a claim on the throne for himself and has signed a contract with us swearing it. He has also brought us information that suggests he may not be the innocent man he claims to be."

"You mean that he admits he killed Father," I said softly.

"No, he was not so stupid," Armand said as he began to pace. He paused and looked at me as he continued. "Although I'm glad you're aware enough now to realize he was involved. No, he was speaking of a plot, a very real plot, to kill the queen. She was nearly murdered last night." I stared at him, my eyes widening. I hadn't noticed anything about Mother this morning that suggested something like that had happened. She'd admittedly behaved very strangely, seemed skittish, but not... what he suggested.

"How," I barely got the word out.

"The usual cowardly way men kill defenseless women," Armand said. "They waited until she'd sent her maids away while she bathed. They thought she wouldn't dare scream while she was so indisposed. They didn't expect her to hit them in the head with her chamber pot." I snickered at the image.

"Between decency and survival, I'm not surprised Mother beat them to save her skin," I said, smoothing over my voice so that it didn't show the intense relief I felt. Someone had gotten close enough to kill Mother, something that scared me more than any attempt on my own life. She had just as many guards as I did and she'd done so many good deeds lately, I couldn't think why no one had warned her. "Is she alright? She wasn't hurt... was she?"

"No, she is perfectly fine, if not slightly embarrassed," Armand said. "But your uncle came to us late in the night and admitted to knowing of the plot through some of his own contacts. He spoke at length with those in charge of your safety and mentioned the word "assassins" several times during the conversation. He also mentioned that these same assassins were familiar with the secret passages in the castle, even the ones to reach your room."

"In other words, he blackmailed all of you into thinking he could somehow protect me if we accepted his protection," I said, scowling.

"We didn't have a choice," Armand said, frowning as well. "You know we must protect you, Christopher, as much as you hate it. We must ensure your safety at all times. And as much as your mother would have fought against the decision, she'd only just been rescued from a most painful death. She was easily persuadable; although I'm sure she's regretting her decision right now. Evelyn does seem to grate on her nerves somewhat."

"Evelyn can't help it," I said, feeling tired. "But Mother already made the deal and she can't go back on it for fear of unleashing my uncle's rage upon her and using her broken word to get more people on his side. I see the problem now. He trapped us all very nicely."

"I am sorry," Armand said. "If I could somehow get you out of it, you know I would. But his information was quite accurate and he hinted to having spies of his own inside the castle. He is prepared to kill you if you do not go through with it, so I suggest you make the most of it." He started towards the door. My eyes widened.

"That's it? That's all you're going to say?" I demanded, jumping to my feet. "Just grin and bear it while my father's brother forces me to do his bidding? He's been trying to get me to marry Evelyn for years now! Just like every other person I know! And how do you think you can stop him from exerting his own influence through Evelyn? Isn't that what we'd always feared?"

"You can use this to your advantage, Sire," Armand said, ignoring my tirade. "Evelyn, if swayed to our way of thinking, can become a great asset to you. I have spoken with others who know her and they say she is mature for her age, generous, and quick-witted. She has survived the politics of court with ease and she will make a good queen."

"Armand," I said, unsure how to strangle him but still force him to listen to me, "I don't think we're talking about the same Evelyn. I've known her for a long time now and she isn't any of the things you've just said. She's obnoxious, clingy, flirtatious, and constantly in the way."

"Begging your pardon, Christopher, but I think you're wrong," Armand said. "Remember that all the people you know, or you think you know, have all been playing a part in this masquerade. Of all the people here, I'm pretty sure you're the last person who knows just what kind of person Evelyn, or any other woman, is. They're pretending in front of you, Christopher. They're catering to what they think you want. If you could get one of them alone without feeling that they need to compete with every other female in the room, I'm fairly certain you'd be surprised just how different these women are."

"I don't want to marry anyone," I said, feeling even more exhausted with this conversation now that we were going through it for the hundredth time. "And I'm pretty sure it would be close to hell for anyone to marry me. Why..." I paused, fighting for the words, "Why can't you just let whoever it is kill me and not worry about the whole thing? It just seems like such a colossal waste of time to protect me all the time."

"We could never let harm come to you, Christopher,"

Armand said, horrified. "You are our king. And I for one could not let anything happen to you. You are too much like…" he paused, scowling.

"Too much like what?" I said, a bit miserably.

"Too much like family," Armand said. My eyebrows shot up at his words. "I'm not supposed to get that close to you. But I've watched you grow up your whole life and as much as you act like a cad sometimes, I couldn't bear the castle without you around."

I stared at him. This was not the Armand I knew. The Armand I knew didn't usually do more than tease me about being too skinny, growing taller too fast for my clothes to keep up, and scolding me for getting his masterpieces dirty. I'd only discovered he was one of the chief spies protecting me by accident. I had a habit of spying on people through secret passages and ever since I'd found out his true identity, I'd made my knowledge plain to him. He'd started updating me on what everyone else knew when it became obvious I wasn't falling for his innocent-servant routine. But he'd never expressed anything but professional interest in me.

"I'm sorry I worry you," I said, thinking of Richard's concern at the funeral. "I'll try not to let you worry."

"So you'll marry Evelyn?" Armand asked suspiciously. "You'll make things smoother with her? You shall have to play the part of willing partner." I leaned back, resting my head against the post. My sense of freedom screamed in outrage at this question, but I understood that it was a question I couldn't treat like all my other decisions. I had to be an adult about this. I had to be, I realized, a king about this.

"Yes," I finally said, though it sounded strained even to my ears. "I will play the part."

"Good," Armand said, breathing a sigh of relief. "That puts my mind at ease."

"Glad it does for one of us," I said glumly. "I don't want to get married."

"Most men don't," Armand said with a teasing smile. "I'll let the others know. They should be pleased." He nodded to my guards and slipped out, disappearing before I could respond. Feeling as if I'd been tricked into admitting some embarrassing secret, I grumbled to myself nonsensically as I went to change. It wouldn't do for my guests to see me wearing the same clothes I'd insisted I so urgently needed to change.

I rested my head against the wall before I moved, gathering my strength for what I knew was to come. I'd made my promise to Armand very easily, but the truth was that playing a part as he'd suggested was not something that would be easy for me. Sure, I could mostly control my facial expressions, a skill I'd been forced to pick up over the years, and I could fake enthusiasm when pressed. At the same time, I'd always had my room for privacy and I could drop the pretense with the servants. Somehow, I knew getting married was going to change all that. I wouldn't have a break from the play, I'd have to pretend all the time, and Evelyn would always be close by.

I would have to be strong, I decided. I'd have to stop putting my opinions out in the open for people to see and I'd have to be convincing about it too. First, I'd speak with Evelyn and let her know I was interested in her, to get things going. Then I'd speak with her parents and smooth things over with them. Yes, I'd pretend it had all been my idea from the beginning. I'd come up with some excuses, make things work. I could do this, I told myself. I'd just follow a plan and everything would work out the way I needed it to.

As I was shifting between shirts, I heard a faint giggle from the corner of my room. Whirling around, I nearly toppled into my shoe section. Evelyn was standing in a ray of sunshine that outlined her in gold, smiling in a way I had never seen her smile. She started walking towards me but her eyes weren't on my face, rather my chest. A sense of dread crept into me as I realized that my brilliant plan was going to be pretty useless the second she opened her mouth.

"I thought you'd been lying about changing clothes. Auntie said I could come here and check on you." So much for difficult-to-reach rooms, came a distant, rational thought. I silently cursed Armand for distracting me only moments before. Had he directed her to my rooms? The sly jerk had just landed himself on my bad list.

"Oh, did she?" I was calmer than I thought I would be. Also, where in the world were my guards? Weren't they supposed to protect me from cruel and unusual punishments? "I didn't know you thought I was a liar."

"I don't," she said. She kept moving towards me, still not watching my face. "You've been nothing but honest with me, as far as I know. But I did want to follow you and talk in private."

"Ah, we'll have the whole day to talk in private," I said. Remembering what I'd promised Armand seconds ago, I tried to relax, knowing that it was showing now, my nervousness. She giggled and looked me in the face at last.

"Well, people will be listening to us, of course. We both know that we're never really alone when we think we are. Your guards and my guards are always close at hand to make sure we're safe at all times, even if it's from each other. No, I wanted for us to talk in private." She purred the word. I felt myself shrinking back. My brilliant plan, I reflected, had a few dents in it if this was going to be Evelyn's reaction.

"Then talk," I said in a squeaky voice.

She pounced on me. I yelped and tried to scramble away but she had me pinned (she was stronger than I took her for) and tried to kiss me. I tried kicking her off but her skirts were in the way every time I tried to squirm away. She started laughing at my attempts to get free.

"What the hell do you think you're doing?" I started shouting. It was… the first thing that popped into my head. Yes, be angry! I told myself. "Unhand me!" I added for good measure.

She stopped and stared down at me in surprise. "What do you mean? Don't you like what I'm doing?" She patted my chest in what I took as a suggestive way. My eyes widened as I started at her.

"I do not like being attacked in my own or any other room, thank you very much. Would you please get off me and behave like a civilized human being?" I said. My voice sounded more irritated than I felt. At that moment I felt extremely disgusted that, 1) I couldn't get this small girl off me and, 2) I was too much of a gentleman to wrestle her off like I wanted to.

"I'm not attacking you," Evelyn said earnestly as she sat up on my thighs. "Momma told me that men usually like it when they can chase women, so I had to be all coy and docile whenever you were around. But then when I went to my room, Momma said that you were a strange sort of man and liked women chasing you so when you went to your room, you were really inviting me to come get you and ravish you." I processed her words slowly, staring at her.

"Do you... even know what the word "ravish" means?" I asked with raised eyebrows.

"Um..." she blushed slightly, "not completely. Momma explained it to me at one point but she was sticking pins in my hair to keep the curls in and it really hurt so I wasn't listening." She touched the back of her hair self-consciously. "I guess I didn't do it right. Momma said you were supposed to say you loved me and then ask to marry me. She said we're supposed to get married because your mom said she'd arranged it."

"Yeah, I know about how we're supposed to be engaged," I said, frowning. I remembered to the way Mother had been quick to distract Frederica at the death festivities (had she been planning this for that long? Had I been the last to know about these plans until Mother couldn't protest anymore?) and how she hadn't let the Rannoch family visit ever since the Skull Juggler's performance. I'd thought it had to do with Richard's early departure but now I realized it probably had more to do with creating a romantic situation for Evelyn and me. I felt bad, thinking of Frederica and her mother's desperate attempts to see me.

"I'm sorry about all this," I said, as much to Evelyn as the absent Frederica.

"You're sorry?" she said with a nervous laugh. She seemed to realize now what a strange position we had fallen into. She was still sitting on my legs and I was half-lying against the wall. "I'm the one that pinned you to the ground when you were changing."

"It isn't your fault," I said, scratching the top of my head so that my hair went everywhere. "We're both puppets in this mess, I imagine. We'll figure out something to do about this." I paused, thinking of something else. "Evelyn, you don't... you're not in love with me, are you?"

Evelyn started laughing. "No! No, I'm not even a little in love with you. You're the nicest and wealthiest of my suitors so far and if I have to marry someone, I'd rather it was someone closer to my age. The next youngest man who's been after me is in his forties."

"Well, I'm glad, I think," I said, feeling a little wounded by her comment. "I'm not in love with you either. I'm not in love with anyone. I don't want to marry right now."

"But your mom already told my momma that we're getting married. They've started inviting guests in secret," she said. I sighed and leaned my head back, closing my eyes.

"That's just perfect," I grumbled.

"It won't be that bad," Evelyn said soothingly as she patted my chest. "I promise I won't mind if you have other girlfriends, as long as we have at least one son and we pretend we're together for the public. Daddy really wants this marriage to happen and if he thought that we were happy, I'd be happy with whatever we do."

I'll just bet he wants this marriage to happen, I thought grimly. Evelyn seemed completely oblivious to her father's corruption and desire for power, otherwise I was certain she wouldn't be so cheerful about the wedding. Dear gods, I'm getting married. When did I start accepting this? I slumped a little, scowling.

"We'll figure something out," I finally agreed. Evelyn sighed softly and smiled.

"I'm actually a bit relieved," she confessed with a little blush. "I love you, Cousin, but I didn't want some ravenous man intent on seducing me at every turn. We can be friends, though, can't we? We don't have to hate each other." She seemed quite excited by this idea. I couldn't help but feel guilty for ever thinking ill of her. Which one of us was seducing the other?

"I'd like that," I admitted. I grimaced. "Do I still have to talk to your friends tonight?"

"Yes, you do," she said firmly. "Now finish whatever you need to do so we can have a wonderful day for my birthday." She clapped her hands excitedly and practically skipped out of my room, exchanging a quick goodbye with my guards. I watched her go with a great sense of awe. This day was only just starting and already I was an engaged man. If only Richard could see me now, he'd get a good laugh out of it.

"Gods, what have I gotten myself into," I grunted as I finished getting dressed. My guards were exchanging smirks when they thought I wasn't paying attention. "And what exactly were the two of you doing while she was attacking me? What if she was trying to kill me?" I demanded. They looked surprised at first, but then one of them laughed.

"Sire, if we had known you were scared to be alone with her, we would have posted a heavier guard," he said.

"We'll make sure to warn you when the cleaning maids come back," the other said, snickering. Oh boy, I thought to myself as I turned bright red. This was going to spread throughout the castle in less than a day. I could just imagine the teasing I'd get whenever the kitchen servants found out about this. With a glare at the guards, I went out to where Evelyn was waiting. Evelyn appeared oblivious to my plight and only observed me and nodded to herself.

"I can't believe I didn't notice before," she said.

"Notice what?" I asked defensively.

"Well, that you're not interested in being married. You always have those women hanging around you at parties and you dance with almost everyone. You seem perfectly calm around all the women I've seen you with," she said. "It just doesn't seem that women surprise you. Then again, I did come out of nowhere. Yes, it makes a little more sense now, I think." I opened my mouth to protest and then promptly closed it. How could I say this?

"I... suppose," I said uncomfortably. "I only dance with them because I have to. If it were up to me, I wouldn't go to parties at all." I fumbled for words that would redeem my masculinity and gave up when I saw the condescending smile on her face. It was hopeless. She'd already made up her mind to "save" me.

This is going to be a long day, I thought.

Interlude
The Three Princesses

Not so many years ago, there were a great many Seers roaming the land. They lived on the road, constantly traveling from town to town. This is the way of Seers, constantly living between places, seeing things that are only sometimes visible and never in the same place twice. At the time, there were a great many Seers who spoke Truth in their visions and told many people about the future.

One day, a powerful king went to the greatest Seer in his land. The king's purpose was to ask the wise man who he should choose to become his new Queen. There were three young princesses from the most powerful countries living in his castle at the time, young women he had selected for this purpose. When he spoke to the Seer, he demanded that the Seer choose the best of the three princesses.

The Seer looked into his great crystal mirror for a long time before he spoke thus: "Great King, come to me tomorrow and I shall tell you of the first princess you have chosen. Bring one loaf of bread for me and a copper penny for the poor."

The King agreed and returned the next day with a loaf of his finest bread and a copper coin, for he liked this woman only a little but found her beauty stunning. When the Seer spoke to the king, he spoke thus: "I see that you do not love this princess. She would make only an average Queen, for she is vain and arrogant. She will give to the poor when she must and she will preserve your reputation with her outward faithfulness, although she will always have one lover other than you. She will bear you only daughters."

The King, struck cold by the future set before him, begged the Seer to look at the next princess he had selected. The wise man agreed and spoke as before: "Great King, come to me tomorrow and I shall tell you of the second princess you have chosen. Bring two loaves of bread for me and a silver penny for the poor."

The next day, the King brought two loaves of his finest bread and a silver penny for the poor, for he liked this princess more than the last. After many minutes of deep contemplation with the spirits, the Seer spoke thus: "I see that you do not love this princess, either, although her great beauty and many skills attract you more than any other. I see here that she is greedy and selfish, and will steal the kingdom's wealth only to shower herself in gifts. She will be a poor Queen, although she will keep her own counsel on matters of state. She will be unfaithful to you and will bear you only daughters."

The King, fearing for his future, knew that this could not be so. He begged the Seer again for guidance and swore that the third princess was far more beautiful and good then all the rest. The Seer spoke as before:

"Great King, come to me tomorrow and I shall tell you of the third princess you have chosen. Bring three loaves of bread for me and a gold penny for the poor."

Determined that this would be his intended bride, the King brought the finest three loaves of bread in all the kingdom and selected the shiniest, brightest gold coin from his personal treasury, for he loved this princess best of all. He wore his wedding garments when he saw the Seer next, secretly delighted with the final princess, for she was by far the most beautiful woman he had ever seen and she was very kind to him. When he gave the gifts to the wise man, he waited impatiently for his fortune.

The Seer said: "This princess is by far the cruelest and most malicious woman in the kingdom. She shall slander your name and ridicule you before your subjects. Her beauty will fade in ten years and she will grow fat and ugly with food and drink. She will be forever unfaithful to you and she will bear you no children at all. She will be the end of this kingdom and a Queen so horrible, none other shall surpass her for many years."

The King was so outraged by this, he struck the Seer and demanded an alternative, for he was half-mad with love for the third princess. The Seer rose from the ground, bloody and anguished, for he did not know how to help the king. He was only a Seer, he could only see the potential futures. He spoke thus: "Great King, you have offered me three options and I have given you three futures. If you come tomorrow with a crumb of bread and a nugget of lead, I shall tell you of the true future before you."

The Great King, miserable with his futures, agreed reluctantly. He returned to his great castle and sent away each of the three princesses, determined to find a suitable wife who would bring him great power.

The next day, the King brought the smallest of crumbs from the moldiest bread in the kingdom, and a nugget of lead so ugly and small, a magnifying lens was needed to see it. The Seer smiled and took the king into his caravan, where the most beautiful girl the king had ever seen in his entire life sat waiting for him. "This is my daughter," the Seer said, "and she is your true wife. You will no longer be a king when you marry her, although she would have made a great Queen. She is kind and generous to all, and she will be faithful to you forever more, even when you have both passed into the Gray Fields. She will bear you many children, many sons."

The Great King fell so in love with the girl that he did not question the Seer's instructions. He immediately left his country with the Seer's daughter and lived a peaceful life away from his responsibilities and his old life.

The Seer, as punishment for uniting his daughter with her true love, was sentenced to a harsh punishment. He was blinded and his tongue was cut out for the Truths he spoke. All over the country, Seers were destroyed and blinded, cursed for all eternity.

It is for this reason that there are no more Seers in the world. The true ones have been hidden to protect them, although some say they will one day return when the King returns from the Gray Fields to reclaim his throne.

- 5 -
The Mourners

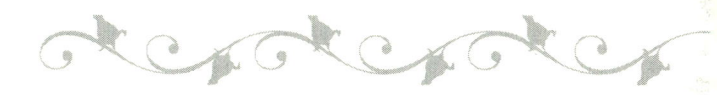

The same ballroom where the Skull Juggler had performed was now refilled with my terrified subjects, who didn't want to be there despite the much-needed festivities. A party was just what they needed to raise their spirits and erase the memory of so much unexpected terror. The foreigners, who were both curious and intrigued by the horror stories people told them about the deceased king's death festivities, were the most daring of my guests. They prodded the darker corners of the castle that no one else would and endlessly questioned the servants for scandalous details of that fateful night. The servants in turn gave mysterious answers, spreading all sorts of wild rumors.

I felt sorriest for the servants who did not gossip while they worked. They had to endure the constant curiosity of my guests. The servants tried to answer questions honestly and quickly, but most of the servants had not been present in the ballroom the night of the Skull Juggler's performance. As I greeted the numerous arrivals, yawning politely behind my hand, I thought back to that night. It seemed so long ago, like a distant dream. I was engaged now, I reminded myself, to a strange girl who tackled me on command and thought we'd make very good friends once we were married. I frowned, thinking how Richard would make fun of me if he could see me now.

Mother refused to talk about the situation at all. I'd tried several times to bring it up, especially about her attack last night, but she'd smoothly changed the subject to the upcoming party. Looking at her now with the knowledge that she had indeed been attacked, I saw the way she looked around the room differently and the way she pressed a hand to her chest as if covering herself. It only served to remind me what kind of life I'd be stepping into if I complied with my promise to Armand.

As I stood there looking around, I wondered if this was what my life would be like for the rest of my life. Would it be like this, living only for the next party, waiting for the next group of people to come speak with me under the pretense of doing something fun, although we always ended up discussing politics because that's what they'd wanted all along? Would I constantly look over my shoulder and make political connections with people I loathed, only to protect myself? My future looked bleak, when viewed through this morbid viewpoint.

The guests faded together after a while, looking all the same to me. Three familiar guests lifted the depression from me for a time, although only briefly. Lady Amelia Rannoch and Frederica greeted us briefly, although with a cold attitude. By the way that Frederica stared at me with hate-filled eyes, I thought she'd been possessed by another person. She'd never looked at me like that before and it took me some time to realize why.

She must have known that I'd become engaged. How she'd found out, and so quickly, I had no way of knowing. Did she know Evelyn socially? I had no idea.

On the other hand, I knew that Nikko Rannoch was highly involved in my protection and was acquainted with a great number of spies that worked to protect me. Perhaps he'd heard the news and spoken to his wife about it. I tried to see the silver lining in the situation: at least now I had one less person to worry about chasing me for my title. This only left a million or so eligible young ladies waiting in the wings, completely unaware that I was off the market at last.

The Rannoch family members were ushered aside soon after they'd arrived by more guests, although Nikko promised to update me on how Richard was faring when I had a free moment. I watched them from across the room as boredom set in again.

"Be a darling and see how Evelyn is doing. It is her birthday," Mother said to me in a sof voice. As I glanced at her, remembering where I was, I noticed an all-too familiar couple approaching us. The Voulders had just arrived. They were a well-known family in my kingdom that lived on the outskirts of Roc. Their ancient house had been built atop a cliff overlooking a large ravine, a ravine that made my land famous. It cut my kingdom nicely in half and, when followed, led to the outskirts of my Eastern lands. In their fairly isolated home, they fancied that they, the Voulders, were the true rulers of Roc. If any travelers from outside of Roc passed by their house, they often claimed to rule the whole land (or so the servants told me).

I hastened to slip away, using one of my guards as

a cover so that they could not notice me leave. Unfortunately, I was too late.

"Please, allow us to see the darling prince before he vanishes," Lady Voulder gushed, having heard the end of Mother's request. "Oh, but he is not a prince anymore, is he? I had nearly forgotten that you were the king now. Oh dear, where is my memory going?" My, but the woman could certainly move when she needed to. She'd practically run from the door.

She grabbed my arm before I could escape, which I realized, too late, I wanted to do very badly. I tried not to show how embarrassed I was. I didn't like people grabbing me, especially women who stared at me quite like that, like I was a piece of particularly tasty meat. I should have gotten used to the look years ago. Evelyn had even looked at me like that this morning.

"I regret that Christopher must go. He should check on his cousin, as it is her party," Mother said, smile still plastered in place.

"But we haven't seen him in such a long time," Lady Voulder said. She even pouted at me, as if I had a say in this overly polite tug-of-war. "The last time we saw him, he was only a little shorter than me! Now look at him, so tall I have to tilt my head back just to get a decent view of him. You can't let him go right this moment; that would be too cruel of you." Mother acquiesced, her eyes narrowing.

When Lady Voulder turned back to me, Mother motioned for some of my guards to get a little closer and hedge in behind Lord Voulder. He glanced back a tad nervously, moving his hands away from his waist.

There was a small, decorative dagger at his hip that he'd worn for most of the years I'd known him. He knew better than to feign ignorance as to its proximity to me. He tried to smile at the guards but they stared at him without blinking.

"Do tell us how you are, Your Majesty. How is your health?" Lady Voulder continued, oblivious to the highly trained army behind her.

Get your disgusting fingers off me before I have you arrested, is what I wanted to say. "I am very well, thank you. How are you?" I said instead.

"I am perfectly fine, although my Robert has been experiencing a bit of indigestion problems, but that's nothing new," Lady Voulder said, smiling blithely. I smiled until it hurt, clenching my fist. Why did everyone come to me with their health problems? Did I look like I could solve them all? "He has such horrible gas. Sometimes I can barely stand to sleep in the same bed!" She laughed. Now that sounds appealing, I wanted to say but Mother was glaring at me. Her and her mind-reading abilities.

"I hope you feel better, sir," I said to Lord Voulder. Robert, so he was named, laughed too loudly and came around his wife, skillfully moving around the guards. I noticed as he approached me that his dagger was gone, as it was now in the hands of a particularly stern-looking guard.

Lord Voulder laughed nervously in the direction of the guards, and then slapped my shoulder as he laughed. I glanced behind him to my guards, who'd moved closer and rested their hands on the hilts of their swords.

Friendly shoulder-slapping appeared to be threatening from where they stood. I was just looking for a friendly exit to get me out of there.

"Listen to that! Polite as a whistle, I tell you. Even calls me "sir." Really, Your Majesty, no need to be so formal! Listen here," Robert Voulder leaned closer, lowering his voice, "some of the other gents have been wondering if you would be so kind as to allow a little hunting expedition in the forest? Against the rules, I know, and not the season, but you must understand, Your Majesty, that the gents are getting awful bored, all cooped up with the women." At the last bit, he gave me a knowing wink. I found myself smiling nervously. "Wouldn't you bend the rules just a little and let us all have a bit of manly fun? Else we're likely to have our manhood fall off and grow into women!" Again he laughed. His wife also laughed.

"Ah... well, I don't really know. It is against the rules," I said. *And I have no desire to be anywhere near you when you get that gas your wife was oh-so wonderful to provide information about. Maybe you and Uncle Albert should head off together somewhere.* "It wouldn't be fair to everyone else," I added.

"Why not the whole city? Begging your pardon, Sire, it's just so dreadfully dull around here during winter." He leaned closer and whispered into my ear loud enough for me to hear and for his spit to tickle my earlobe. "Besides, we boys need a chance to get away and have fun with some of the ladies outside of the town, if you catch my meaning, Sire." And he wriggled his thin eyebrows suggestively.

"Well, in that case, I'll take it into careful consideration," I said, biting off the sarcasm as I rubbed my ear. I wanted to laugh in his face. What woman in her right mind would let you anywhere near her? Lady Voulder laughed without hearing what her husband said. From my reaction, she thought it was a joke. On second thought, maybe you could find women crazy enough to sleep with you, I thought.

"Really, Your Majesty, your son is such a peach," Lady Voulder said to Mother.

"Yes, a real peach," Mother said beautifully. She was smiling, not at me, but at Robert. I think she did hear what he had said. And she obviously didn't want me going anywhere with him any time soon. That was the beauty of having a vengeful mother – she shared her bitterness with people other than me.

"I should check on Evelyn," I said, remembering Mother's excuse for me to escape. "I promised I'd chat with her friends," I said and smiled charmingly at Lady Voulder. "It's her birthday today." Lady Voulder melted into a puddle of cooing and aww-ing.

"He's so adorable. Oh, I wish I could just take him home with me," she said. For a moment, I was scared that she would really grab me, stuff me under her skirts, and run away with me. I even took a step away from her, glancing nervously at my guards. She restrained herself, much to my relief. She did, however, grab my cheek and shake my entire face.

I've never been one to have a lot of baby fat so she was practically shaking my cheekbone instead of my skin. When she finally let go, I smiled more out of pain than pleasure. I could feel the skin burning from the affectionate gesture.

"Thank you, madam. You are too kind," I said and nodded to Robert as his wife giggled. This was the perfect opportunity to get the heck away from them and I took it. Freedom! a treacherous voice in my mind screamed. I looked around and saw Evelyn waving frantically for me to join her with a group of giggling and gawking girls. Run while you can, fool! Run for your life! I replaced my smile and took long, confident strides towards them, nodding to the people I passed. Acting, I reminded myself. I was acting a part and the character I was playing had to smile, had to meet his future bride with loving eyes. It sickened me, but I did it.

"I thought I should come rescue you from the invalids, my lady," I said to Evelyn as I drew closer. I flashed her cloister of friends a smirk that made them all giggle. At first, Evelyn didn't seem to recognize me. It's true, I'd never approached her in this way before, but she seemed to relax the second I was there. I smiled at her in a friendly way, winking when the others weren't looking. She giggled in return, her smile widening.

One of her friends surprised me when she smacked my arm playfully with her fan. It was a lovely fan, I could see, and it was scented very faintly.

"Your cousin is positively naughty, Evelyn," she said. "Save you from the invalids indeed!"

"Is he? I never thought him to be so," Evelyn said. There was an edge to her words as she placed her arm through mine. Evelyn's bubbly attitude from earlier in the day seemed to have vanished in the presence of her friends. Perhaps it was just this particular friend. Oh well, I reflected, I'm trapped now. I will let things happen as they must. Now... what would the character I was playing say? Something charming...

"You don't know me very well, Cousin. For all you know, I could be very naughty," I said. There was a collective sigh among the girls before more giggles. I realized what I'd said and wanted to smack myself. It had sounded far stupider outside my mouth than in my head.

"If you were," Evelyn said, falling into stride, "then we should have plenty of fun tomorrow when we go out riding." The girls giggled at her comment and I bravely kept grinning although I felt my cheeks get a little pink.

"Mother suggested that we have a toast for you and that I make a speech. What should I say?" I asked, expecting her to tease me again. This might be bearable, I reflected. If it was pretend, Evelyn and I could have a lot of fun.

"You are wicked," said fan-girl. She hit me again, gentler this time. Her fan also happened to linger on my arm. "You know very well that you shouldn't tell her if you're going to make a toast."

"Well, what do you suggest I say," I said.

Looking at her now, I noticed that she was obnoxiously beautiful, perfect so far as I could see. Most people like that always mean trouble, at least when they flirt with me the way this girl was flirting. She was blonde and pale and dressed all in blue. She should have been dressed in red. Or not dressed at all for that matter, considering how much of herself she was revealing. The sexual undertone was all in her voice. The sultry voices the kitchen girls imitated and the husky speaking Evelyn had tried on me earlier were amateurish compared to this girl. She obviously knew what she was doing.

"Naughty, you shouldn't ask me in front of Evelyn. She won't be surprised if I reveal all my secrets to you. And besides, I have to make a speech for her myself and anything I say might compromise her surprise. That won't do at all," she said as she shook her fan at me. She probably knows what the word "ravish" means, I thought distantly. I opened my mouth to reply but Evelyn tugged sharply on my arm and moved closer to me. Ah, territory. I know this game. I calculated a different approach, now knowing that Evelyn and this woman were going to clash.

"Cousin, this is my friend, the Lady Raquel. She hails from Duhn," Evelyn said in a constricted voice.

"Ah, enchanted to make your acquaintance," I said. Raquel smiled serenely and tossed her long blonde hair. I straightened a little, trying not to look down from her face. Huh, maybe this was going to be harder than I thought if women were going to look like that around me.

"Evelyn, he is too darling," she cooed, perfectly aware of the way she was affecting me, at least physically. "He seems like the perfect gentleman, just like you said. Might I steal him away to ask him some questions about Roc? This is such a fascinating kingdom. Did you know that in other countries, they copy the fashion in

Roc? You have one of the most popular styles in all of Duhn."

"No fair, Raquel," one of the other girls interrupted before she could continue. "You know very well you have to let us meet him before you distract him with all of your gossip. Besides, he's a man. He doesn't care about fashion any more than a stone cares about the sky." The new girl wasn't nearly as beautiful as Lady Raquel but she was radiant in an entirely different way. She looked completely different than every single woman in the ballroom, clearly not giving a hoot who saw her heavily tanned skin or her frayed gown. She flashed me a predatory grin. "You can't always leave us with second helpings."

"You never complain when you go for my leftovers," Raquel said in a much softer voice. Ah, there was history between these two. I kept this in mind as I smiled in a pacifying way.

"Ladies, there is no need to fight. I will remain here so long as Evelyn wishes it so," I said. I smiled at her too and felt her grip on my arm loosen. She was smiling at me in more of a thankful way than out of pleasure for my words. "Evelyn, who are your other friends? I'm afraid I didn't catch their names."

"This is Lady Mystiza from the Emerald Isles and this is Lady Katarina from the Southern Lands," she said. A mousy brunette with large blue eyes, Lady Katarina, smiled from behind Lady Mystiza. She was taller than all the other girls and the most easily ignored. I felt a little stupid for not even noticing her until Evelyn pointed her out. She seemed the most uncomfortable and out-of-place in the group.

"I have a good friend in the Southern Lands," I said to Lady Katarina. She blanched when I started talking to her, looking down at her shoes.

"O-Oh?" she said softly.

"Richard Rannoch, he and I grew up together," I said. She gasped, looking up immediately.

"You know Richard?" she asked excitedly.

"He's my best friend," I said, feeling far more comfortable talking about a friend. Lady Katarina practically glowed, her smile was so wide.

"I met him when I was five," she said breathlessly. "He's very... nice." I knew she hadn't wanted to say "nice." She said "nice" as if it meant "mind-blowing and amazing," or "god-like in every way," or even "wonderful and he is the love of my life, I want his babies." I smiled faintly when I saw how pleased she was, talking about him.

"If you see him again, tell him Christopher says hello. He's there right now, studying I believe," I said conversationally. "Don't believe anything he tells you though. He's so full of himself, it's a wonder he can fit through doorways." Lady Katarina giggled, her eyes wide with admiration. I need not have lathered on the charm so strongly, she was practically drooling on the floor. I silently thanked Richard for giving me something to talk about.

"Is it true that you are the king of this whole castle?" Raquel asked before the other girls could say a word.

"Yes," I said, regretfully looking at her. It was always easier to talk about Richard than it was to talk about myself. "Perhaps, at another time, I could show all of your friends my kingdom." I glanced at Evelyn to see if this was what she wanted me to say. She was beaming back at me.

"Isn't he such a darling?" she cooed and hugged my arm all the tighter. Again with the darling. I hadn't been anyone's darling since I was three years old.

"He is, indeed, a wonderful cousin," Raquel said.

"And a good friend, it seems," Mystiza said, beaming at Lady Katarina. Mystiza's gown, I noticed, seemed a bit strained in places, as if the gown had not been made for her. Although Raquel had the breath-taking beauty, there was something about her calculating behavior that made me prefer Mystiza and even the shy-looking Katarina.

"I've met your other cousins in the Emerald Isles," Mystiza said. "They're a bunch of stiffs, if you don't mind my saying. You physically resemble them a little, your cousin Bernard more than the others. He's no fun though, always hunting in the mountains in the mainland."

"How is Bernard? Did he tell you that once, when we were racing horses when I was six years old, he pushed me over into a creek? He nearly killed me. I hope you punched him in the face," I said. It took me (and the girls) a minute to realize that I had actually said this out loud. Maybe I was getting a bit too comfortable. "I mean, er, I hope he's doing well." Katarina giggled.

"Well, we did have a wrestling match," Mystiza said with a rakish grin. "As a matter of fact, I tossed him into a creek. He cried like a baby."

"Very unbecoming of a thirty-year-old monarch," I

said, trying to hide a grin. Raquel stared at us with a frown on her pretty face.

"I'm afraid we can't all be as uncivilized as Mystiza," Raquel said. "Such behavior is suitable only for children, is it not Your Majesty? I'm sure you do not go around tossing family members into creeks anymore. Mystiza still does such things, you see. But poor dear, that has more to do with her upbringing than anything else. Did you know that she was raised among the lower classes?"

I exchanged a quick glance with Evelyn, trying to figure out how I was supposed to react to this statement. What would the character I was playing say to that? I could sense the tension in the air and I knew that if I opened my mouth, something especially stupid would come out of it. I settled for looking mildly uncomfortable and waiting for someone else to react.

"Shut up, Raquel," Evelyn, surprisingly, was the one who said this. She glared at Raquel with a loathing I'd never seen her possess. I glanced between the girls, noticing their tension reach palpable levels, and the way they looked at each other across their fans.

"Oh, you didn't tell him?" Raquel said delightedly, "That is too bad of you, Evelyn. The king has a right to know who he converses with in his own castle!" she turned her attention to me, her eyes devious. "Mystiza isn't really nobility, you see. Not really. Her parents didn't want her after her birth, something about her appearance must have offended their sensibilities, I except, and so they—,"

"Shut up, Raquel," Mystiza hissed, her eyes widening.

"—abandoned her in the mountains in the most frightful of places, I have been told, probably so that the wolves could eat her. Imagine her fortune when some farmers happened upon her several days later. Lucky for her they did, although I can't say they were very lucky themselves. It turns out she was a great disappointment. When they found her, they thought the Gods had sent her to them, can you imagine—,"

"Raquel, I'm warning you," Evelyn said quietly.

"—and then, when she was fully grown and came to clean the king's stables years later, one of the servants noticed that she happened to hold a strong resemblance to the prince of the household. And there you are! Instant nobility!" she finished quickly, a smug grin visible around her fan. I stared at her uncertainly, wondering what she expected me to do with this information. I felt uncomfortable looking between the girls, trying to determine what best to do.

"Excuse us, Christopher," Evelyn said in a dangerous voice. She grabbed Raquel by the upper arm and dragged her away. Judging by the grimace Raquel flashed me, it must have been painful.

I watched the other girls, Katarina and Mystiza, glance in my direction and hurry after Evelyn. I scowled as they left, trying not to roll my eyes. Female behavior was something entirely beyond me, even more so when it was the behavior of royalty. None of the servant girls I knew seemed as cruel or petty as the women I was normally forced to associate with.

I tried to ignore the heated whispers from their direction, shifting my attention to watching the people dance nearby in their over-the-top, brilliantly colored gowns and tuxedos. Boredom followed soon after.

Interlude
Rosemary Seeds:
A Love Story

Rosemary was once a beautiful peasant girl who lived with her family beside a large castle. Her little hut was so small, the wind could not howl in it and the sun could not show his face within, for there was barely enough room for people, let alone these glorious elements. Rosemary lived only with her tired mother and her feeble grandmother. Her father had died long ago from the green fever. Before he died, he gave his daughter a small box of dirt with a single rosebud growing inside. "This is a magical garden," he told his daughter, "and it will protect you always."

The day of her father's death, the magical garden began to make flowers of such beauty, Rosemary could hardly look at them. Beautiful blues and violets, yellows and honey-colored petals, strong, beautiful stems of such green that she nearly cried. The garden allowed Rosemary to pluck these flowers and sell them at the market, creating more the very next morning. This is how Rosemary survived, selling the garden's flowers at the market while her tired mother darned her torn clothing and her feeble grandmother swept the floor of the tiny hut. It was a good life and Rosemary was happy.

The special thing about these flowers that made Rosemary famous throughout the land was how beautiful their enchantment was. Famous heroes and lovers came to buy her flowers, sometimes falling in love with her for a moment as they paid in gold coin, other times falling in love with their beloved more deeply. Although she did not know it, faeries and changling creatures oftentimes bought her flowers and praised their beauty to the magical creatures of the forest. She was famous in many places for her flowers.

She became so famous, in fact, that she spoke to her little garden one day: "Please, little garden. I need more flowers than usual for the market tomorrow. My poor, tired mother has great pain in her hands and my feeble grandmother groans in her sleep. Please help me sell more beautiful flowers so that I may buy medicine for them."

A soft male voice said to the girl: "Come tomorrow morning and I shall have flowers for you. Only remember, do not pluck the rose, for I live there and will die without it." For you see, the little garden loved Rosemary a great deal and could refuse her nothing.

Rosemary eagerly agreed and went to her bed and slept closest to the garden beside her tired mother and feeble grandmother. She dreamt of the garden's voice and the beautiful flowers she would sell.

The next morning when the sun touched the door of her little house, Rosemary leapt out of bed and rushed to the little garden. She gasped in delight when she saw ten beautiful white flowers in the little garden. When she touched the petals, she gasped in delight. They were made of ivory, a material she'd only ever seen from a distance at the market.

The single rose at the center, the garden's home, had blossomed slightly so that the tip of the bud resembled a pair of ruby lips. Rosemary remembered the garden's gentle voice the night before and kissed the petals of the red rose, as thanks for working so hard for her. She gathered the ivory flowers and went to the market.

She sold every one of her flowers that day to the richest, most beautiful dressed people she had ever seen. Only one buyer wore the skin of a wolf and looked at her with strange eyes. This man was not human and frightened the other flower girls who walked the streets beside Rosemary, but Rosemary did not fear him. She gave him one of the sweet ivory flowers and smiled at him so gently, the wolf-man smiled back and gave her a small pouch of medicine for her tired mother and feeble grandmother, for he was a faerie who knew the pain of humans.

A beautiful prince came to her last and bought the loveliest, sweetest flower of all and instantly fell in love with Rosemary.

"Come to my castle tomorrow," insisted the prince. "I want to show your beautiful flowers to my mother and father." Rosemary was at once delighted and disappointed, for the flower the prince held was the most beautiful she'd ever seen. She was determined to please the prince, for she was a kind girl and wished only to make those around her happy, so she agreed.

That night, Rosemary soothed her tired mother and

her feeble grandmother with the medicine of the wolfman. They cried their happiness and gave her the Seventh God's blessing. Feeling happy that her mother no longer felt tired and her grandmother no longer looked so feeble, Rosemary returned to the little garden and whispered to it: "Thank you for the lovely flowers. But please, I need more, and far lovelier than ever!"

"Were not the flowers I gave you lovely?" the gentle voice came as before, sad and beautiful. Rosemary rested her head on her hands, staring at the lone red rose, for she had plucked the rest.

"They were breath-taking," Rosemary cried, her eyes widening. "I loved them all dearly!"

"Why, then, do you need more? I am tired. I spent a great deal of magic making you such lovely flowers," the voice said.

"Oh, I am so sorry," Rosemary said, feeling ashamed of her request. "But you see, the prince wished to have more lovely flowers for the king and queen. I do not want to disappoint him."

"Do you love him?" the voice asked sadly.

"Of course not!" Rosemary said with a little gasp. "I could not love a prince. I am only a peasant girl. And I cannot love him, for I do not know him."

"Very well," said the garden with great reluctance. "I shall make you three very special flowers. So long as you let me rest tomorrow."

Rosemary thanked the garden and gently kissed the red rose, noticing that its soft petals had bloomed yet further than it had the day before. She went to sleep on the floor close to the garden while her mother and grandmother cradled each other on the bed. Rosemary dreamed of the garden and especially the red rose.

The next morning, she gasped in delight. There were three perfect, beautiful jade roses in the garden. Rosemary hastily took them and thanked the garden. She donned her nicest dress, washed her face, her hands, and her little feet before she went to the prince's castle. She was made to enter through the servant's entrance, for try as she might, no one could mistake her for anything but a peasant girl selling flowers.

When the prince saw Rosemary with the lovely jade flowers, he urged her to come to the throne room. Before this, he gave her a beautiful gown spun of the finest silk and embroidered with beautiful jewels, for she was too plain to meet his parents in a peasant's plain dress.

The king and queen marveled over the jade flowers and fell in love with Rosemary, as the prince had done only the day before. They decided then and there that Rosemary should wed their son the following day. Rosemary happily agreed, thinking how her mother and grandmother would no longer live in poverty and pain. The king and queen insisted that Rosemary return the next day with a beautiful gift for her new husband. They thought she was a grand lady, and not a peasant girl, and knew nothing of her tiny hut. They only loved her as they saw her.

Rosemary returned home that night with joy in her heart and excitement in her stride. She did not notice how her new shoes and gown grew dirty from the filth of the street, for a peasant girl could not possibly worry about such things. She had trouble standing in her little house with her enormous gown of spun silk. Her mother and grandmother were glad to see her and that night, they were gladder still to sleep on the dress, for it was softer than their hard bed.

Rosemary went to the magical garden and whispered: "Please, little garden, I know you are weary. But please make one more flower for me, more beautiful than any other. I am to marry the prince tomorrow and I need a wedding gift for him."

The garden did not respond at first, so tired was he who made the flowers. He said: "But you promised I could rest... and you said you did not love the prince." The voice was sad, for he loved Rosemary more than anyone else in the world.

"Please," Rosemary said, "I must marry him. My mother is so tired and my grandmother is so feeble. I must take care of them, and I know the prince will do this for me."

"I will not do it," the garden said crossly, "you do not love him." Rosemary pleaded and begged but the garden refused. With a sob, Rosemary wept over the garden and fell asleep beside it, convinced that all hope was lost.

The next morning, the prince came to her house to wake her. He was disgusted by the dirty road and the tiny house, too small even for a horse's stall. When he went inside, he felt even more disgusted when he saw that the beautiful gown he'd given his bride-to-be was now filthy where her tired mother and feeble grandmother slept. He tore the gown out from under them and raged at them, terrifying the old women. They ran out of the little house crying. They ran to the ends of the earth, surely lost to all who loved them.

Rosemary awoke with a start and when she realized what had happened, she grew furious with the prince and ordered him to leave. In her own little hut, she ruled more strictly than any princess. She would not marry a man who treated her family in this way.

The prince, feeling shame for angering his bride in this way, thought of how best to console her. He noticed the little garden at once, for there were two flowers growing there. The first was the most beautiful red rose he'd ever seen, perfectly colored and fully bloomed. The other flower, of greater interest to him, was a beautiful flower made of pure gold.

As Rosemary had slept, tears on her cheeks, the garden had relented. He loved Rosemary and could deny her nothing. With his last strength, the garden created the most beautiful flower he'd ever made before. He put all of his love for Rosemary into his work. It was this magic that made all who touched the flowers fall in love with Rosemary, for the garden loved her so.

Knowing that the gold flower belonged to him, the prince plucked the red rose from the garden in the hopes of soothing his lovely bride.

Rosemary screamed in horror when she saw what he'd done. The gold flower shriveled and sank back into the blackening garden. In the castle, the king and queen cried out in horror as their beloved jade flowers wilted and shrank to weeds in their hands. Only the red rose remained beautiful and sweet.

The spell on the prince lifted and he no longer loved

Rosemary. He left the little hut, dazed and ashamed, although he knew not why.

Rosemary cried over the red rose as she felt her heart breaking. She pressed her cheek to the soft petals and begged forgiveness for her treachery. She longed for the garden's gentle voice and kind love. Her salty tears soaked the rose and it vanished, only to be replaced by a handsome man. Rosemary's eyes widened as the man took her in his arms and kissed her. He was a faerie like the wolf-man, only he had been under a spell. He'd watched and loved Rosemary since her birth. Her tears had broken the spell that imprisoned him in the flower.

"I will love you," the faerie promised, "forever. Be my bride."

Rosemary agreed and they went together to a land filled with flowers and nature. The wolf-man, as a wedding gift to the couple, brought back Rosemary's bewildered mother and confused grandmother. They and all the faerie folk who'd ever bought her flowers came to the wedding and all were happy.

It is for this reason that rosemary seeds, when planted in a garden and nurtured with love, always bring your true love.

- 6 -
Revenge

I was becoming more involved in my people-watching, wondering (and dreading) if I should ask one of the eager-looking women to dance, when the lights in the ballroom slowly dimmed to glow like gray fireflies. Candles flickered across the floor in a dazzling display of gold and harsh white, so dim that no one could see anything at all. Some people started to make excited and frightened noises.

There was a sudden burst of fire in the center of the room. Most of the women close to me screeched and leapt back into the protective arms of their male relatives and lovers. I froze, thinking the Skull Juggler had returned to the castle. I searched for Mother in the darkness, unable to see anything but the mask-like faces when the fire burst forth again. Could it be that she was the one behind the Skull Juggler all along and she had made him return to kill me? Was this a clever distraction for a murder, like my father's?

I realized immediately after this thought that it wasn't the Skull Juggler's performance at all. I'd been stupid and paranoid to leap to such a far-fetched idea.

The performers were visible only through bouts of flame, and even then it was confusing because they were twin sisters. Fire-breathing twins – I think that was the first time we'd ever had such performers. Mother had really outdone herself, selecting perhaps the perfect distraction for the guests.

The performers swept each other into a serpentine embrace as they danced across the floor, breathing fire in unison seemingly by magic. I watched, trying to figure out what form of sorcery or machinery they used to create the fire effect. The crowd gasped when they felt the heat of the flame close to their faces and screamed in delight when they saw their companions in the light.

"I hope you are enjoying the performance," someone said beside me. I nearly jumped out of my skin and only fractionally relaxed when I realized it was just Frederica. She must have been standing beside me for some time. She smiled faintly at me, a gesture that looked more gruesome by the light of the fire.

"It's unique," I said, forcing myself to calm down. It was only Frederica Rannoch, obedient Frederica who used to follow Richard and me when we were kids. Frederica, who let us cut off her braid when she was four because she said she wanted to be a boy, like us, so she could play our adventuring games. She always wanted to be the ugly old man with the gimp leg when we played pirates and she insisted that such a man would not wear braids. Her mother had nearly killed us for letting her. I smiled at the memory, relaxing at last.

"I like fire," Frederica said offhandedly. "Of all the elements, it is my favorite one. There is something so primal about fire... People don't really understand its destructive nature. They forget how much it has helped humanity in more than just practical ways. Did you know that in some cultures, the priests worship fire?" I glanced at her, waiting for the burst of flame to see her expression. When it came, I felt nervous standing next to her. She had a strange smile on her face and an expression I'd never seen before. She looked as if she wanted to play with the fire. She looked as if she wanted to grab the performers and... I didn't know what. My intuition told me I didn't want to know.

"It's something so passionate... so alive," she said in that strange, slightly excited voice. "I've always thought fire is the physical manifestation of passion. Passion for life...perhaps."

"Ah, yes..." I said, concentrating on the performance. We were in a somewhat secluded corner of the ballroom and away from the main crowd. The lights seemed different here and Frederica too seemed different, in a completely creepy way. I very much wanted to get out of there but I didn't know how to do it politely. Frederica was my best friend's sister and, for as long as I'd known her, she was determined to marry me. If she knew about my upcoming nuptials already, perhaps I should have expected this strange behavior from her earlier.

Looking at her unguarded expression, I was reminded of my conversation with Armand earlier in the day (it seemed like so long ago). He'd said that every single woman I'd ever known who was trying to marry me was also playing a part, just as I was now. No woman was behaving as her true self, but instead pretending to be what they thought I wanted. I realized that it wasn't just Evelyn I didn't know but also Frederica. She'd changed over the years, I knew. As a child she'd enjoyed being friends with me because she admired her big brother more than anyone else in the world. Now though, she was grown. She knew exactly what she was doing and, I realized, she'd been an extremely good actress.

She didn't seem to be pretending for my benefit anymore. Was she really this creepy?

"I could write a poem about this," she said. Maybe not that creepy, I thought, remembering how she'd gone through a phase some years ago when she wrote very awful poetry. Richard insisted the terror had come to an end, but it seemed she still dabbled a bit in lyrics. I tried to relax, focusing on this little bit of normalcy. If a girl could write poetry about stupid things, she couldn't be as creepy as I'd thought.

"I'm sure you could," I said, just to say something.

"I've heard a rumor that you're getting married," she said nonchalantly. I looked away, clenching my fists to keep from cursing. Part of me still hoped she hadn't heard about it, but obviously she had. With a growing sense of dread, I wondered if she'd told anyone else. Was this strange plan of my uncle's meant to be kept a secret until I was already married? Was I supposed to be quiet about the marriage?

I took a deep breath and glanced back at her, hoping she hadn't seen the look on my face. I need not have worried, she wasn't looking at me. She was staring at the performers with that same strange, interested expression on her face. "I offer my congratulations on your upcoming wedding," she said. "I'm sure you know that

I've been pursuing you for years now." I frowned, unsure what she was getting at.

"I know your mother has been interested in me... you've both been trying to get my attention for years," I said slowly. She didn't seem to be listening, but I knew she was. I had the sinking sensation that she was listening to things I wasn't even saying. That was a level of scary I didn't even want to touch on. The way women seemed to intuitively guess what men (in particular what I) thought was unnerving. "I'm sorry, about not telling you about the engagement. I didn't mean for you to feel... as if you weren't good enough. I was only doing what I thought was best," I said, letting the words tumble out in the hopes of blocking whatever mind-control, women's intuition thing she was doing to me.

"I offer my congratulations to the lucky girl. She must have fought very hard to win you," she said stiffly.

"You make it sound like I'm a prize," I said, frowning. I wanted her to look at me so I could figure out what she wanted. She wouldn't look though, only gazing at the performers.

"Oh, but you are a prize," she said, finally glancing up at me. I could see the hate so clearly in her eyes, I almost thought she'd burn a hole right through my forehead. Her entire body was shaking as if she was suppressing sobs, something that really would have frightened me if she started crying.

"I'm sorry you feel that way," I said uncomfortably.

"No need," she said, composing herself. "We all know that marriage to you is a competition and the best woman will win. Which is the very reason I have told every single eligible female in this room that you need to be married by the end of the week and that you are currently in search of a new bride. I have modestly stepped aside, you see, because I have my eye on a bigger prize. Their mothers will be speaking with you soon, as the Queen has left the ballroom only a few minutes ago." With that little catastrophe deposited nicely in my lap, Frederica left my side and mingled with the crowd. I stared after her, my eyes widening with horror.

Mother was not in the ballroom, just as Frederica had noted, as did the mothers of eligible young ladies all around the room. These particular mothers knew that the Queen was the only person of any authority who stood between their daughters and (royal) marital bliss. I soon felt caged in by the people edging closer to me in the darkness and I made my escape before the next burst of flame.

Silently cursing Frederica for being far more vengeful than I'd ever thought her capable of, I hurried out of the room through the servants' passages. These would confuse the women chasing me and would afford me some time to think of a better place to hide. There was no use staying at the party now, not if every single woman thought I had some sort of doomsday attached to my marriage. I knew what desperate women were capable of (both Evelyn's behavior in my room earlier that day and Frederica's behavior just then proven it to me). Mother was generally a great barrier between me and the army of women desperate to live a happily-ever-after scenario. Without her there, I shuddered to think what they would do to me.

I paused in the kitchen, breathing a sigh of relief. I

grabbed an unsuspecting pastry from one of the baskets and waved to the cooks and servants. Abigail glanced up briefly from juggling several bowls, her nose powdered with flour. She huffed a greeting at me and then turned back to what she was doing, probably thinking I was escaping from the party while no one could notice me. I heard uncomfortable whispers from the direction of the ballroom and picked up my pace, quickly walking out of the kitchen and through the castle towards the gardens. As it was somewhat out of the way of the guests, I thought I'd be safe there.

I slipped into the garden and relaxed as I made my way towards the quietest corner. This was usually the best place for me to relax and enjoy the sweet smell of the beautifully colored flowers, although I would never admit this to anyone. It also reminded me of a fairy tale I'd read years ago about a magical garden and a love story, but for the life of me I couldn't remember it now.

I took great pride in the upkeep of my castle's garden. Most gardens I'd ever seen in my brief travels were exotic, filled with foreign plants and elaborately designed landscaping. My gardens were more natural in that they held native plants, beautifully-colored flowers that only grew in the bitter cold, some with a reputation for being outrageously expensive and rare. My favorite ones were the flowers that were unusual, such as those that were poisonous or had some special talent for defending against their predators. There were even some flowers here that only bloomed in the dead of night or only during moonlight hours.

The bit about moonlight should have been my first hint.

I realized soon enough that someone had noted my escape from the ballroom and that I'd been followed. I wasn't even half way through the entrance before I noticed several lovely young ladies posing dramatically by the roses, draped over the fountains, and reclining against the gazebo. The women managed to appear both lovely and devilish in the torchlight, carefully glaring at each other when they noticed me standing there with my mouth hanging open. This was no good. I shifted my direction through a lesser known path and practically ran to the stables, the only non-romantic place I could think of that would afford me some time to escape.

During the long trek to the stables, I became half excited by my progress. I'd been cooped up in the castle for so long without seeing the sky except through my bedroom window, I'd nearly forgotten what it felt like to stretch my legs. Part of me gave in to the drama of the whole situation, allowing my excitement to build so that I ran instead of walked, even uphill and over rocky ground.

A young boy lay fast asleep in the first stall that I crashed into. He jumped into wakefulness and yelped when he recognized me.

"S-Sorry Your M-M-Majesty," he gasped as he stumbled towards a random horse. He saddled her with a speed and skill I had never before witnessed. He saddled a young colt, a horse I'd never ridden before, with shaking hands. The horse was disconcerted and skittish at the boy's heightened emotions, and the fear showed in the way the horse snorted and tossed his head from side to side.

"Don't worry about it, just hurry," I said, peering around the corner to see if I'd been followed. The excitement of the chase made me feel stronger and exhilarated in a way I hadn't been for weeks. The boy's eyes widened, probably from the impassioned expression on my face, and worked faster. I mounted my horse as soon as I could, quickly wheeling him out towards the forest. The boy stumbled after me, panting hard.

"Thank you for your speed, I will remember it," I said, still looking around.

"Are you b-b-being pursued, S-S-Sire?" the boy said desperately. "Sire, I can f-fight for you! P-Please, I can f-fight!" My frantic glancing paused and I looked back at him. He appeared to be about twelve years old, with large round ears and faded red hair framing a strong face. His skin was starkly white and he'd clenched his hands around a pitchfork twice his height, his entire body shaking so hard that he looked about to fall into pieces. Despite his obvious terror, he seemed determined to face whatever I asked of him.

"Have no fear, I can handle them," I said, thinking of the hungry look the mothers had given me. "They cannot be fought, only eluded and escaped. I will be back later," I joked, trying to lighten his fear. At that moment, I saw movement at the corner of my eye. Whether it was the boy's panic or my own, it doesn't matter now. A thrill of excitement went through me and I urged my horse forward into the forest without a second thought.

INTERLUDE
The Tin Shoes

There was once a princess who fell in love with the local blacksmith's son. They met every day in his father's shop and they loved each other very deeply. Although the blacksmith's son swore to love her for his whole life, he knew that he could never marry the princess. The princess would not listen to his reasoning and clung to her dream of one day marrying her beautiful suitor.

One day, she was forced to marry a widowed king. He was a kind man but three times her age and more of a grandfather than a husband. The princess, now a queen, secretly dreamed of the blacksmith's son every night. She fantasized about what her life would have been like. She imagined washing his clothes, making his dinner, kissing his hands every night. She thought of his smile as she prepared for parties and balls in her new kingdom, she thought of his eyes as she tended her children, and she thought of his soft voice when her husband made love to her.

The king eventually died, for he was very old when he married the young princess. The queen's children were grown now and the queen realized with growing excitement that she was finally free to do as she wished, for the first time in her life. She knew what she wanted most in the world.

She traveled to her father's kingdom and went to see the blacksmith's son. When she came to the old shop, she was surprised that the blacksmith's son was now the blacksmith. She gaped at him, shocked by how handsome and strong he had grown.

"How may I help you, My Lady?" he asked. The queen felt self-conscious in the face of such a handsome man. She was aware that her beauty had faded over the years and her face was lined with cobwebs of wrinkles around her mouth and eyes. She could not speak to him looking as she did now, no longer beautiful.

She was so frightened, she ran away. She traveled back to her father's castle and locked herself in her old room. She sat on her bed, crying over her cowardice. How many years she had dreamed of seeing him, and he was so much more handsome than she'd ever imagined! And she, old and brittle now, she could not hope to be beautiful enough for him!

Later that night, the queen was surprised by an unexpected visitor. The blacksmith came to her with a gift in his large hands, his eyes gentle when he saw her.

"I did not recognize you before, dear lady. I had thought I would never see you again," he said. "You have grown even more beautiful than my imagination." The queen's heart fluttered and she hoped against hope that he still loved her as she did.

"I was so nervous, seeing you again," she confided.

"I could not understand why," he said, "until I spoke

with my wife. She reminded me of the beautiful lady I had once loved." The queen felt her heart break at that moment. He had married. He did not love her anymore. The blacksmith opened his gift and gave it to her. "I made these for you for your wedding gift, so many years ago," he said.

The queen took the tin shoes with care. They were delicate and beautiful, a wonderful gift. She knew she would never be without them.

"I loved you," the queen said.

"I loved you, too," the blacksmith said sadly. "But I fell in love with my wife. I could not pine for you forever. You are a queen now, and I a lowly blacksmith. This is the natural order of things."

He left her soon after, happy to return to his family. The queen, filled with rage and pain, remembered her fantasies of the blacksmith during her years of marriage and motherhood. She remembered his eyes, his smile, his gentle voice, and something inside her broke.

From that day onward, she wore the tin shoes every day. Whenever a woman is spurned by the man she loves, you can hear the queen's tin shoes at night as she paces, remembering what she has lost.

- 7 -

The Last Breath

I am a seasoned rider but I rode an unfamiliar horse that panicked at every noise in the forest, noises that seemed magnified and constantly behind us. He ran blindly wherever he could find an open path, becoming even more panicked when tree branches scratched or slapped his hindquarters. I managed to rein him in after wrestling with him for some time, slowing his run to a canter and then a trot. He snorted hard to catch his breath but my growing calm seemed to help him over time.

Now that I was out in the forest, I took the time to look around. It was difficult to see anything in the darkness but my eyes eventually adjusted so that I could notice little things. I could make out the pale, distinct landmarks in the forest that had once guided people looking for the castle.

The main road had only been constructed several hundred years ago. Before that, people who came to Roc needed some sort of sign to find the castle among all the trees. I was told that in other countries, most castles were not surrounded by such a dense forest as mine was. We lived in virtual isolation, I was told. It was something I knew peripherally but understood only now that I was outside. This far from the castle, I felt almost as if there was no castle.

I could see the chipped stones along the ground in various places, beside twisted trees and pools of standing water. These stones were the markers I'd been seeing as I traveled deeper into the forest. The more stones clustered together, the closer I was to the castle. There were only some here and there this far into the forest and I thought distantly of how vulnerable I was right now. If anything were to happen to me, no one would be able to help me. I was utterly and completely alone.

Instead of frightening me, this thought made me feel more powerful. I didn't have to worry about disappointing anyone out here. If I fell off my horse and broke my leg in a ditch, it would be my own stupidity that got me killed. If someone attacked me, it would be just me and that other person. No one even knew where I was, not even the stuttering stable boy.

"Serves them right," I mumbled to myself, thinking of Armand and his promises. It was enough to make me glad I'd left the ballroom early. Mother could be as annoyed as she wanted later and yell at me for endangering my life and blah blah blah. I was going to enjoy the night air and walk about the forest for as long as I wished. This would be good for me, I decided. How long had I been trapped in my room? How long had I contemplated how best to strangle myself with my own socks? Being outside helped me breathe normally for the first time in forever. I couldn't stand the way everyone hovered over my every move, worrying that every little thing I did could result in my eminent death. Being outside now was the only relief I could think of and I was going to enjoy this no matter what happened anyone said.

Unfortunately, the more I thought about relaxing, the less I relaxed. I kept glancing back at the castle thinking of all the people who would be looking for me as soon as my disappearance was discovered. Armand would wonder where I was, Mother would most certainly panic about my disappearance, and even Evelyn and her friends would wonder. I was sure even Frederica would be confused that I'd simply vanished after the tense conversation we'd had. She was obsessive and creepy but she wasn't stupid.

When I realized I was only going to get more frustrated the longer I was outside of my guards' protection, I decided to go back home and deal with whatever punishment I'd get for leaving for however long I'd been gone. I could just imagine what everyone would say when I got back. I thought, without pleasure, of the torrents of women who would want to speak with me the second I set foot in that ballroom again. The night was young, after all, and there were still guests arriving the last time I'd checked.

Just as I'd resigned myself to my fate and had turned my stead back to the castle, something landed on my horse's hindquarters. I had a chance to note that this something smelled horrible and had a tendency to hiss.

The terrified horse bolted straight ahead, his head held high as he dashed past trees and over fallen logs, too terrified to hear my screams for him to stop. I tried to rein him in but three branches successively smashed into my face, dazing me, smearing my saddle with sticky blood. I almost lost my grip on the horse's mane just then, though I tried my hardest to hold on.

I just managed to slow him down when the moonlight reflected off a lake just in front of us, perfectly circular and clear as glass. The horse instinctively swerved to avoid the water that seemed to have materialized without warning, an obstacle he hadn't anticipated anymore then I had. The horse lost his footing on the slipper rocks and stumbled, flinging me clear off his back. The saddle hadn't been fastened correctly, I noted in some distant part of my mind. I was flying, cart wheeling in midair, clear across the edge of the lake and into the waiting embrace of the dark water.

The water seemed to open up and crash around me all at once as I sank, down into oblivion. I didn't slow down, just dropped like a rock. Bubbles gradually drifted to the surface without me, much as I tried to swim after them. The clothes, those damned party clothes I'd worn to the party, weighed my limbs down so much that I couldn't even thrash properly. My eyes burned from the water but I could still see a strangely pale-gold shape swimming around me, giggling at my turmoil. I tried to grab at it but my fingers touched nothing at all and I continued slipping deeper into inky darkness. It no longer felt like water but more like ink, slipping around me as I slid lower.

My vision cleared as I sank, and I became distantly surprised at how enormous the lake was from the inside. The edges slanted downward and then disappeared so that I felt as if I was falling into a second, darker lake within the lake. The change in temperature shocked me and I started thrashing harder, panic making everything more claustrophobic, more frustrating and helpless.

Surely someone was coming to help me. Surely I wasn't going to drown.

My feet touched the sandy bottom and I sank until I was lying flat on my back, the sand hungrily swallowing my legs and arms so that only my chest and head were above the sand. My lungs burned and I clenched my eyes at the sharp pain this caused. I knew that the second I tried to breathe, the water would kill me.

The image of the inky water, the reflected moonlight at the last moment, the laughing creature; the images came together in my mind and I knew all at once where I was. This was the Widow's Lake, famed for the number of men who had drowned here over the decades. I'd always thought it was a legend the servants told to scare me. Now, as I gradually stopped fighting for air, I knew that I was doomed to become just another ghost story. I would become one of the dreaming dead. I would lie in the black sand, half-buried like this, forever, just staring up at the surface of the lake and mourning the life I'd never get to live.

So... this was what it felt like to die.

It wasn't as bad as I had anticipated. I thought that I would have experienced more pain, or maybe my life flashing before my eyes, or journeying to the Gray Fields where all souls went, or maybe just something that felt like falling asleep forever. Instead, I felt more alert and awake than I ever had before. I heard the sand swaying to the current of the lake, which was strange since I didn't think lakes could have currents, especially lakes that seemed so peaceful on the surface. I felt my body relax more and more until my every movement was synchronized with that strange current, swaying. My breathing gradually slowed and then stopped as I slipped from living into... something else.

I was dead now, I could feel it. I could feel the tug at my soul to pull me out of my body but I couldn't move. I was stuck. Far away I could hear the soft laughter of old men and the gentle giggles of young women. The cold sway felt like a cradle for my tired bones, the freezing in my head and body a sharp contrast to the warmth I could feel in my hands.

The surface of the lake glowed high above me. It continued to glow until a face appeared. It was a beautiful, soft face. It was a woman's pale face. Her eyelashes were white and her lips were the palest pink I had ever seen, almost unnoticeable. Her eyes slowly opened and she smiled down at me, her irises frosted white.

'Sleep, my love, and let your soul rest here with me. I will protect you now,' a voice whispered soothingly in my ear. Or was it my mind? I couldn't tell where the face came from, only that it was very close to me. The woman giggled and her image disappeared from the surface of the water, taking on a corporeal form close by.

Her glowing, white body floated down to me through the water, the long tresses of her hair floating behind her like ripples in a pond. She smiled wider and came to rest on top of me, her face lowering so that she could speak against my lips.

'Do not fear me. Give in. Stop fighting me,' she said. She disappeared and reappeared above me, floating a few feet away. Her lips curved into a smirk as she held out her hand. In it, a sinister glow beckoned to me and I recoiled.

'Give in and this body will be yours, always. Give in and sleep, my pretty little King,' she purred to me. I stared at her, at her lovely, oval face and the promise in her hand, and I knew that this woman, this monster, was evil. Worse still, I was now trapped in her graveyard.

interlude
The Widow's Lake

Once there was a young, beautiful witch who lived alone in her cottage at the edge of a magical lake. She was a good witch who helped many people. It did not matter how far she had to travel or that those she helped often had little money to offer her. She used her good magic and knowledge of herbal remedies to heal plants, animals, and any humans that she came across, regardless of social class or wealth.

When she reached her seventeenth year of life, she began walking regularly to the local village, intent on selling her herbal remedies to the sickly people who were unfortunate enough to catch the green fever. Only magic could destroy this curse and she was happy to offer her services in exchange for a single rosemary seed, for witches had a great many uses for seeds.

When she nursed the sick in the healing houses, she met a young doctor. He came from a large city many miles away from the village and he used all of his great knowledge to help those who had the green fever.

The two healers fell in love and were married soon after. The witch soon converted to the religion of the

Seventh God and began to pray to her husband's god, she was so in love with the young doctor. They moved into the witch's cottage in the woods after their marriage.

Life between the two lovers was blissful. The young witch was too weak and frail to bear a child but she had long since spoken to her husband about adopting some of the orphans in the village, a proposition that appealed to the gentle doctor.

The two were euphoric living as they did until the tragic day the doctor grew ill. Instead of risking his wife's health, the good doctor isolated himself from her. He escaped his home and went deeper into the woods, bringing with him only a single rosemary seed to remember his beautiful wife. He died very painfully, cold and alone, in the woods where he thought his wife could never find his body.

But she did find his body.

Instead of burying him, as was customary in that country, she dragged his corpse back to her cottage. The witch continued life as if nothing had changed. She convinced herself that her husband answered her when she called him. She heard his voice when she slept beside his rotting corpse and smiled when she picked herbs in her enchanted garden, although no rosemary grew there anymore.

The village people eventually discovered what had become of the kind doctor and, more disturbing still, what his distressed wife had done when she found his body. A group of well-wishers, who had always respected the work that the witch and the doctor had done together, took it upon themselves to do something about this poor, disturbed Widow. She couldn't seem to move on; her husband's life was not the end and yet she acted as if she would shatter at the very mention of his death. This was not the way of the Seventh God and the people worried her betrayal of their god would hurt her in the afterlife.

These kind-hearted people stole the Widow's decomposing husband while she was away one day and held a quiet funeral for him beside the lake. They extended the ceremony so that the Widow would discover them. They believed that seeing her husband's body in this way, in a coffin as it should have been, would give her closure for his death or at least shock her out of her madness.

The Widow screamed curses at her old friends when she saw her husband's body in a coffin. She ran into the lake and drowned herself, taking with her those foolish enough to bar her path.

Thereafter, the lake became her lake and no one dared go there. Those unfortunate enough to stumble into it discovered they too had to die and become the Widow's husband. That is, until a new soul fell into the lake.

- 8 -
ESCAPE

No opportunity presented itself for escape from the Widow's Lake until the day that another poor wretch fell into it.

I was staring up at the surface, as I often did, when I felt an explosion all around me. A black explosion formed high above me and a body came falling down, down into my cold grave. Long, elegant ripples painted his descent, trumpeting his arrival. I felt my legs loosened from the sand and I pushed myself out of the ditch without thought.

The Widow swam up to meet the body sailing down towards us. I kicked hard and propelled my tired body toward the surface. What remained of my constraining cloak remained trapped in the sand (the main reason for my having drowned in the first place). I also left behind my shoes, an absence that made me painfully aware of how cold my toes were.

Nothing stopped me. I swam past the Widow but she didn't see me. She was giggling and whispering coyly against the paralyzed man's ear, stroking his cheek as she swam down with him into her tomb. I paused when

I was close to the surface, torn for a moment. I thought to save her newest victim, as I wished someone had done for me, but the reasonable voice in my mind told me that he was already lost to the world. My choices were to either attract her attention and get pulled back down, possibly forever, or get my freezing behind out of the water and onto dry land.

I broke the surface but didn't draw in a breath. I didn't need to, what with not breathing for so long. Paddling to the shore, I pulled myself out of the water and over the slippery, perfectly round stones that had been the very cause for my having been stuck in the Widow's home in the first place. When I was out, I noticed for the first time that one of my rings, a gold one my father had given me years ago, was still underwater where I had left it. A pang of frustration swept over me but I wasn't about to jump back into the water to get the ring. I would rather get blisters all the way back to the castle and miss it forever so long as I didn't have to go back in there.

I stared up at the night sky. The moon had a large ring around it, glowing down on me, welcoming me back to the land of the living. A lot of time had passed, I knew, and the moon only reminded me of this fact since the moon had been different the night I died. This passage of time meant that, when I returned to the castle, people would think that I was long dead and never coming back. Well, they were in for a nasty shock, weren't they? I considered looking down into the water to catch a glimpse of the man who had fallen in, but I didn't dare go near it, not even out of respect for the poor wretch who had saved me. It may have been a scout from my castle looking for me, or maybe a peasant picking herbs for his family.

Stumbling to my feet, I trudged towards the path leading back to my castle. There was a quiet disturbance of water from behind me and then vehement coughing. I heard something wet and heavy crawl up from the center of the lake and dog paddle to the edge. Turning very slowly, I expected to see the colorless Widow staring back at me, furious that I had dared escape her. I prepared to run, as much good as that would have done, but I didn't see the Widow. Instead, I saw none other than the Skull Juggler, sitting on the edge of the lake, dripping wet and coughing. He was no longer wearing his skull mask, I noted with interest.

He looked strange in the bright moonlight. His skin was almost as tan as his skeleton mask had been pale. His hair dripped into his face, obscuring his strange gray eyes as he knelt on the stones, coughing up lake water. I stared at him for a long time before I hurried to his side and dragged him away from the edge, amazed that I was even helping him. I barely knew him and yet here I was, risking the Widow coming out of the water and strangling me with my own intestines. He glared at me and shook my arms off his shoulders, clearing his throat as he climbed to his feet. He glared at me for a long moment more before shaking the water out of his hair.

You look like a drowned cat, I thought, though I didn't dare say this out loud. Something in my face must have betrayed my thoughts because he growled,

"You don't look much better, Your Royal Highness." He tromped back to dry land, shaking his legs to get off the last bits of clinging water. I followed him (because where else was I going to go?) and paused at the sight of a horse waiting patiently by some trees. I knew there was something strange about the horse just by looking at it, though I couldn't make out what it could be from my location.

I stayed on the nice familiar moss for another minute before I dared approach the Skull Juggler. With his back turned to me, I could now recognize the body I had seen the Widow dragging through the water. Something about the Skull Juggler's taste must have displeased her though, for her to spit him back up so quickly. He had to be the one I had seen; I doubted another moron could have fallen into the lake so promptly after him. When I reached his soggy side, he was drying off with a cloth, which he tossed at me when he was done.

I ignored the cloth, eyeing him wearily. I looked over him more closely, noting some unsettling details. He wasn't wearing a shirt or shoes, something that made me think perhaps he hadn't just fallen into the water by accident.

"I saved you, you know," the Skull Juggler said, making me lift my eyes from the ground where his shoes were mysteriously absent. "I feared she might have already ensnared you in her spell. Luckily you weren't too far gone to get away when the opportunity presented itself. I hadn't planned on her being so attached to her new toys."

I instinctively clamped my mouth shut, fighting the

anger that would come out. It occurred to me, staring at his bare feet, that no one knew where I was. How had the Skull Juggler discovered that I was trapped underwater, or that I was even in this area of the forest? It wasn't as if I was near the castle. The last anyone had heard from me, I'd been safe in the castle for Evelyn's birthday party. The last time he had seen me, I was in my castle among my subjects for my father's death festivities. He didn't seem in the least bit surprised to see me, although his attitude reflected that he'd stumbled upon me by accident. Although even this behavior was strange, as I should have been dead judging by what he'd done to my guard with the whole black rose debacle. There was nothing to suggest that I would be here of all places.

"She likes to cling to the new people," I said without a clue whether it was true or not. I just wanted to say something so that I wouldn't feel so angry anymore. "I'm surprised she was so attached to you," I said.

"Of course she was attached to me; she thought I was her lover. Those particular ghosts draw their existence from the life force of the living," he said with a snort. At the mention of ghosts, I remembered that I too was dead and that I had no desire to eat a living being's life force. I didn't even know what a life force looked like, much less what it tasted like.

The ridiculousness of the statement made me laugh. The Skull Juggler arched an eyebrow derisively in my direction as he pulled a shirt from the pack on his strange horse, jerking it over his head. "You shouldn't laugh quite so hard. There are creatures far worse in the forest that would eat more than just your essence," he said.

"As far as I'm concerned, I don't have an essence anymore," I said, snorting with laughter.

"Don't be stupid, Prince," the Skull Juggler said as he dried out his pants and his hair before reaching for the shoes lying on the back of his horse. "You have no idea what you're talking about. Gods, I hope you won't be this obnoxious once we get on the road." The laughter chocked in my throat and dread filled my stomach like lead.

"What did you just say?" I demanded.

"Speak that way with me again, Highness, and I will gladly throw you back with the fishes," he said as he shoved his feet into his shoes.

"You presume to come along and rave that you somehow saved me from the Widow," I began venomously, "when it was, in fact, you who made this "deal" with her so that you could watch me get killed just for your benefit. Then you prance around, pretending to be my master, as if I had begged you to do me this wonderful service, killing me and then saving me, only to make me your slave. You demand I respect you and lick your boots the second I come crawling out of that blow fish's pond, because I would somehow remember your kindness when it was you who dared interrupt my father's festivities and kill my subjects. The last time we met, you tried to kill me. I have no doubt you had a hand in it this time!" I was shouting in his face by the end, my words half insane. I had thrown all of my suspicions and wild accusations at him more because the shock was wearing off and the fear of what I had just experienced was taking over. The Skull Juggler paled, eyes widening.

"I had nothing to do with your death," he said calmly.

"Pardon me if I find your every spoken word a testament to your tongue's inability to speak the truth," I screamed in a rush. He stared at me for a heartbeat, processing my words.

"I didn't!" he insisted, looking towards the lake nervously. "I had intended to scare your horse into the forest so that we could speak in private, without the interference of your subjects or guests. I didn't intend your death." I froze in my angry tirade, realizing what he'd admitted. He scared my horse? What did he do? When did he scare my horse?

"You're a liar," I hissed, even angrier than before. "I don't believe a word you say."

"Whether I killed you or not is irrelevant. You are under my charge now," the Skull Juggler said smoothly. "You shouldn't worry about it. Where we're going, you'll be able to make a new beginning. No one will know your history or where you've come from. You can't go home." He turned away from me and whistled softly. The strange horse came towards him, or I thought it was a horse until I saw it closer.

One of the ears looked as if it had been chewed off and it was missing its right eye and half of its face. I could see the muscles working and, worst of all, the smell of decaying flesh rose up so strongly that I gagged and turned away.

The horse was dead, I realized. I also realized that arguing with a man who could get away from the Widow and rode a dead horse was not someone I wanted to have anything to do with, much less scream in his face. The lake water popped in one of my ears, waking me from my paralyzing thoughts. I knew I couldn't stay there anymore.

The Skull Juggler had his back to me as he saddled his strange horse, still speaking although I didn't pay attention anymore. I waited a few seconds and then tip-toed to the edge of the water, carefully skirting the branches and leaves that looked as if they would give me away. He continued talking, absorbed in his task (and probably amused by the sound of his own voice).

"– you'll like the warmer climate, I'm sure of it. It's just so bleak and miserable here all the time, you'd think the gods hated this place. And the damnable bugs here get into everything. I'm going to get some herbs for the trip so that our horse does not decide to begin the more gruesome stages of decomposition along the way…"

I slipped away into the forest and hurried back the way I thought my castle had to be. I used the landmarks, the chipped stones littering the ground, to find my way back. Soon my legs were moving without thought and I lost track of time. I wandered for what felt like hours, stumbling in the darkness and breathing so hard I thought I would hyperventilate. When I realized that I was breathing again, I paused long enough to test it. I didn't need to breathe, I reflected, but it felt more comfortable so I continued doing it.

After such a long time in the forest, completely lost,

I worried that I would never find my way home despite the landmarks. Wouldn't that have been wonderfully ironic? I escape the lake just to get miserably lost in my own forest, destined never to return home. I could just hear the Skull Juggler laughing at me wherever he was.

My feet were aching by the time I reached the edge of the forest. Brambles and sticks tore my arms and I picked at the wounded skin, wincing when I felt sticky liquid on my arms. I looked back at the trail of blood left on branches and fallen leaves along the ground. In the light of the moon, my blood looked black and demonic. I shivered and leaned against a tree to look at the damage I'd done to my feet. They were coated in grime with pieces of grass stuck between my toes, but there were no wounds. I touched the heel of my foot but felt no blood, only pieces of crushed wood and snail shells. It unnerved me to see that walking for so long with the sharp stab of branches in the night had no visible effect on my unprotected feet. I decided to ignore it for now and focus on getting home.

I turned back to the castle and hurried towards the kitchens. I knew where the servants' entrance was and at that time of night, no one was going to stop or question me. The questions could wait until I got some rest. All I wanted to do was see my room, my things, the familiar objects that could hopefully make the nightmare seem less real. I wanted to erase every memory creeping up on me now – the endlessness, the cold, her face.

INTERLUDE

THE BOOK OF HORN BY: JACOB FIRE

CHAPTER 6 "THE ACT"

Introduction

There are a number of abilities that correspond to a necromancer's arsenal of skills and power, all of which are directly related to the mode of their death. Necromancers refer to their deaths by using the term "the act" or as their "rebirth." For academic purposes, I shall refer to it as "the act," as this is the more literary term:

A necromancer's "act" can only occur under highly specific and rigid rules:

1) He or she must have a strong affinity and predisposition for magic during his or her lifetime, well before his or her death.

2) Another necromancer, referred to as the "senior" necromancer, must be in the near vicinity during The Act so that the younger necromancer, referred to as a fledgling, may be bonded as The Act occurs.

3) The mode of death must be very specifically magical in nature. The soul must be trapped within the body and remain ensconced within the body for a duration of at least one year up to one hundred years at the most.

This final point will be the focus of this chapter and is, in many respects, the most fascinating topic for magical theory and discussion.

The Act

Although people have discovered innumerable ways to kill each other, there are four basic categories for necromancers. These categories, called The Four Factions, also have their own specific forms of governing themselves as well as their own leaders as liaisons between other factions as well as the living. The four factions are: fire, water, air, and earth.

Fire: This form of death is perhaps the most violent and painful way to die, and one of the rarest forms of magical death. It includes such death as a house fire, explosions, gun shot wounds, and anything else that can be linked in some ways to fire (some of the ways this applies surprise even seasoned necromancers). Individuals who die through this form must have an especially powerful magical predisposition before death and the senior necromancer must be close at hand during The Act. The body, if it survives, must be cared for directly by the senior – this is the only form of necromancy that requires the senior to be directly involved.

These unique individuals have a form of offensive

necromancy that is both dangerous and awe-inspiring in its power. The magic must be controlled at all times or the soul will burn out faster, usually killing everything around it at the same time. Fire necromancy is highly powerful and used in war whenever necromancers become involved. It is also the most painful form of necromancy to endure, in some circumstances. It is for this reason that the fire faction is the most highly-regulated and the most rigidly controlled group of necromancers.

Noteworthy People: Pierce Fire, Diana Fire, Jacob Fire (the author of this book).

Water: This form of necromancy is one of the hardest to master and understand, both because of the complexity of this group's training and the often flabbergasting hierarchy of seniors within the faction itself. These deaths include drowning in a lake, but also include such illnesses as pneumonia, rain-related accidents, and in some cases of torture. Whereas fire necromancy is both offensive and driven by instinct, water necromancy is a more defensive power driven by intuition and foresight. The more sensitive a necromancer, the more likely he or she will develop unique and powerful skills that no one has ever heard of.

It is for this reason that this form of necromancy has more room to grow than any other form, although these necromancers begin their training as the weakest of all other necromancers. The senior also has very little involvement during The Act, making the bonded relationship between fledgling and senior one of equal partnership, something equally unique. This faction is notable for being the most mysterious and secretive of all the other factions.

Noteworthy People: Marius Water, Sylvia Water, Cassandra Water.

Air: Intuitively, one might think that there could not be a faction of air necromancy, as the human mind does not normally associate certain forms of death with air. This group is, incidentally, a highly populated one. These magical deaths include strangulation (hangings, for example), some forms of drowning, and some particular cases of tuberculosis. The senior is fairly involved in The Act, unlike water necromancy, as he or she must protect the body of the fledgling after The Act, for a number of years (this number varies, although we know that one hundred years is the longest known resting point). There is often the danger of decomposition or scavengers so bodies are generally stored indoors or underground.

Their magic is somewhat unreliable and unpredictable, like the people who wield it. These necromancers tend to be the most empathic to the living, as their magic does not manifest as strongly as in fire necromancy, for example, and they usually act as the agents of communication between other factions and the living. Their form of government is thus the most similar to the forms of government of the living. On an interesting side note, this group also contains the largest number of criminals.

Noteworthy People: Pike Air, Harrison Air, Lana Air.

Earth: This group is one of the most feared of all necromancers because these people tend to be physically deformed when they awaken from The Act. This group is mostly made up of people who have been buried alive or killed by magical creatures closely associated with nature, such as elves or faerie folk.

Their magic is one of the most powerful in that they must use various magical tools to channel their abilities. The magic itself is not so powerful but, through their use of talismans and artifacts they create, they can be the most formidable of enemies. The black rose, for example, can be used by all necromancers, but it is the earth necromancers who can actually grow the plant and harvest the flower. They can also concoct elaborate and complex spells and potions for the living to use. They have a governing body that usually regulates trade more than individuals, so they tend to be closely allied with the air faction.

Noteworthy People: Bryce Earth, Yolen Earth, Meg Earth.

For more information on each faction, refer to the Table of Contents or the glossary at the end of this book.

- 9 -
HOME

I'd lost hope of finding home at a certain point and cuddled up against an especially large cluster of stones when I saw it through the trees. I was already lying down staring ahead of me, glumly thinking of home, when I saw it. Stumbling to my feet, I ran the last few hundred feet and fell all at once through the underbrush. There it was right there all along. I nearly cried in relief, half running, half limping towards the castle doors. My mind raced with all the things I'd thought were impossible moments before: I would see my room, I would see my bed, I would see the kitchen servants, I would see Mother, and Armand, and maybe even Richard had come home! I would have been happy just to see Frederica. In fact, I'd probably have kissed her if I saw her. At that point, I was ready to marry anyone I was told to marry, and I would have done it with a huge grin on my face. Just so long as I didn't have to go back to where I'd just been.

As I approached, I started looking more closely around me. There was something very wrong with the castle, I noticed. The light from inside seemed to come from the wrong direction or to fall against the ground in an eerie, unusual way. I noticed this and looked around, making sure I wasn't being followed by the Skull Juggler. It would have been just like him to sneak up behind me and give me a real heart attack. Silently cursing him under my breath, I paused on my long trek to the kitchen door when I noticed something very strange by the stables.

I thought to walk beyond it and get inside before anything else bad could happen but I was too curious. I paused in my half-run and changed direction, following the meager light to the edge of that strange structure that didn't seem to belong. As I came closer, I started piecing together images that still didn't make sense.

It was a stone building about a story high, although it was slightly taller than that because of the carefully arched roof and the thick walls. I stopped a little away from it, staring at it. For some reason, it made me feel even more disturbed than I had been at escaping the Widow's Lake. There was something so wrong about the building standing beside the stables. I looked at the stables in question, trying to understand what it could be. I wasn't normally this slow, but the difference didn't make sense when I realized what it was that was bothering me.

The structure stood right in front of the entrance to the stables, a place it should not have been. There was no possible way any person, let alone a horse, could come out with such a huge building in the way. Because of the building's proximity, part of the stable shouldn't have even been intact either. The building's roof had a sharp, invasive roof that stretched out to clip the side of the stables cleanly. Instead of destroying that part of the stables, however, it seemed only to go through it as if it wasn't real. The two buildings seemed super imposed on each other and this was the reason I couldn't understand what I'd been seeing. It didn't make any sense, the way the buildings stood so closely together, even touching, and yet both were completely intact.

How the masons had built this other building, I had no idea. How could this new, ugly structure stand so close to the stables when there shouldn't have been room to build anything so close? Even worse, where did they put the horses? How were the carriages going to get out? Was there another entrance now? I came closer, inspecting the connecting buildings. As I gazed up from under the two joined roofs, I understood it less. There wasn't nearly enough light to see by but it still didn't look right.

The sense of dread grew in the pit of my stomach and I turned away, feeling very strange about the building. When I'd reached the kitchen door, I looked back. Looking at it from afar, I decided there was something else that was architecturally wrong with it. The building looked as if it should have stood alone on a hilltop somewhere, surrounded by nothing more than trees or grass. It didn't look as if it should be part of a greater structure, such as the castle. That was part of the point of castles – it was not just the castle that was close by. Castles had various buildings attached to them, such as the stables and the servants' quarters, but this building did not fit like the castle's connecting buildings did. The stone was all wrong, the color did not even attempt to blend with the buildings alongside it, and it served no purpose that I could ascertain. It was too strange, I decided, to worry about at that moment.

When I reached the kitchen door I was looking for, my hands trembled as I opened it a crack and slide inside. With one last suspicious look towards the forest, I closed the door and leaned against it with my eyes closed. Images slithered behind my eyelids as I stood there. I remembered another time I had stood here like this, trembling and crying, with my uncle (another uncle – my mother's brother) pounding on the door. I had been in trouble for scaring his horse, just as I was in trouble now. The memory made me terrified all over again.

I moved away from the door and walked to the main study. I pressed the brick in the fireplace, which opened the hidden passage as I had done so often in my life. I ducked automatically under the collapsed beam, something I had also done all my life, and proceeded into the darkness. I felt safe here, recognizing every groan of the castle and the soft purr of my feet on the floor. The outline of a door was visible minutes before I was anywhere near it and I sighed as the doorknob turned. Being locked out of my room would have been too much for me, I think, and that small miracle made my limbs feel a hundred pounds lighter.

I went through the door and nodded tiredly towards my guards, as I always did. I didn't recognize them but I attributed this to the recent problems with the necromancers and the political uprising that Mother and Armand had been so worried about. Despite not knowing who they were, I thought it best to acknowledge their presence in my room in as polite a way as I could. It wouldn't do to be impolite with them when they were risking their lives for me constantly. Who wanted to protect an unpleasant miscreant anyway?

One of the guards harrumphed as I passed but in the next moment he stiffened, his eyes going so wide that the whites framed his gray irises. The other guard started breathing very quickly and grew extremely pale.

While they stood by the door gaping at me, I went to my dressing room and peeled off my pants and left them on the floor, grabbing some dry ones. As I was concentrating on untangling myself from my shirt, the frustration of my situation was taken out on my clothing. One of the guards, the second one I had noticed, cautiously approached the entryway and stared at me. I wiggled around to glare at him through the neck hole in the shirt, fighting back an angry comment at his codfish-like appearance.

"Do you mind giving me some help?" I asked as politely as I could, given the circumstances. I couldn't help the tired bite of sarcasm in my tone. He gawked at me, his large mouth hanging open like a jack-o-lantern. His sagging cheeks were pockmarked like an orange and only heightened the comical image. His armor was a little tight, judging by the folds of skin lumped under his armpits, but the metal was clean and in good condition. I softened my expression seeing the genuinely confused look on his face.

"I apologize for my rude behavior and my abrupt appearance. I know I have been gone for a while," although I don't know how long, I thought silently, "but I'm tired. I couldn't sleep where I was and if you would be so kind, I'd really like to get some rest before I explain to everyone what I know of what happened. So could you please help me get out of this deathtrap?" I wiggled my arms helplessly to demonstrate my plight. The guard carefully composed his features and approached me.

"Right... er, what's your name? And how did you get up here?" he mumbled as he helped peel the shirt off me. I shivered as my wet back was exposed to the air and hurried to grab some dry, warm clothing.

"This is my room," I said. "And I came in through the passage in the main study on the ground floor. I could have taken some other passage but that was the closest one to the kitchens. I didn't want to see anyone yet. If it's all the same to you, I'd prefer you didn't mention anything about me until tomorrow. I don't know how much more of this talking I can take." My eyes started closing all on their own and I felt my head tilting forward. It all came together, the constant fear, the endless thinking, my escape, and my agonizing trek through the forest with the pain of my bare feet keeping me awake. I had nothing to keep me awake now. The guard, sensing this, took my arm and led me towards the bed, still looking perplexed.

"Oh..." whispered the guard still by the door. His face was pale and his left hand rested on the hilt of his sword, which rattled in its scabbard. He held a handkerchief to his nose, breathing in deeply.

"What's the matter with him?" I mumbled to the

guard at my elbow. He glanced at his companion worriedly but shook his head.

"Oh... well, Carlyle is scared of ghosts," he said. I glanced at the guard, Carlyle, who whimpered when I looked at him. He pressed his back against the wall and stared at me as if I were something disgusting and terrifying that had snuck into his shoe. I smiled in as friendly a manner as I could and crawled into my bed, burying myself in pillows. The familiar feel of my pillows soothed me in an instant.

"If it makes him feel better, tell him I'm scared of ghosts, too," I said. I hesitated with the blankets half way to my chin. Did I want to ask him some questions before I slept? I had been gone for a long time, if the strange building beside the stables had been any indication, but how long was the question. I kept getting hints of things but I couldn't put all the ideas together in a coherent way that made sense to me.

I thought to ask about the people I knew. Was Mother alright? Had there been any attempts on her life again, as there had been right before Evelyn's birthday party? Was the Rannoch family doing well? Had there been any news through Armand? Speaking of which... where was Armand? Why wasn't anyone rushing off to get him? I wished that he was there to tell me what was happening. I knew he would have told me what was going on. He would have understood what was happening and told me exactly what I needed to know.

The thoughts in my head were panicking me, I realized. I was breathing harder and clenching my fists to the point of pain. I thought of other people to ask for. Was Evelyn alright? Was Richard home from studying? What about Frederica? What about... everyone? Abigail? Maggie? All of the kitchen staff? Even my advisor Mathew, who I never thought of... how were all of them?

It was too much, I realized, far too much to think about just then. I had other things to worry about. I had to focus on what was going on around me in the present and I could only do that if I rest first. My thoughts were too slow right now to concentrate on much else. Things that should have been obvious to me were too complex to get through in a normal amount of time and I was too worried about unimportant details, such as the strange structure by the stables and how the carriages were possibly going to get out. I even thought about how angry Mother was going to be if she knew that no one would be able to do their job properly, since the carriages couldn't get out.

There was no gradual sleepiness or moments of alertness as I lay on my bed and relaxed. The instant I closed my eyes, I fell into a deep sleep. I would remember later what they said before a dream took me.

"You don't think it's... you-know-who," one voice whispered fearfully. "Geoffrey, you don't think it is, do you? I mean, my dad always insisted he'd be back some day. He said there was no way he'd just abandon all of us like they always said he would. Do you think it's him though? Do you think he's a ghost?"

"I don't know," the other whispered back, a note of awe in his voice. He and his friend were huddled by the door but I could hear every word they said. "He seemed real enough to me."

iNTERLUDE

Taken from the Archives of the Charnel Family
Personal Accounts from the Historian – vol. 61, page unknown
Side Note Beside Longer Printed Narrative

- ... one of the most popular rumors has circulated primarily among the castle servants who were closest to the king before his disappearance. According to my interviews, they believe that Christopher might have been lost in the catacombs instead of kidnapped and murdered, as is the next most popular assumption. This theory is not so far-fetched as I'd initially surmised. They, the oldest servants, recall an instance years ago when Christopher, at the age of six, did indeed get lost in the catacombs. Christopher was lost for three days wandering the catacombs, crying out for help. He did not always know the path to his room. According to my most valid sources, it was the tailor Armand who discovered him at last close to the cellars. It is unclear how he managed to reach the cellars through the path he described to others later. All that we know for certain is that his relationship with the servants changed af-

- 10 -

The Struggle

I dreamt that I was in an open field. The tips of grain were golden and swayed like little dancers in the wind. When I opened my eyes in the dream, I was lying on my back and basking in the sun. I didn't move for a long time, enjoying the warmth and the breeze, soothing away all of my fears and worries. The clouds overhead seemed suspended and lazy.

"It must be nice, not to feel the fishies nipping at your ears," a voice said above me. I jerked and twisted around to look behind me but there was nothing there, only more flowers and an endless landscape. I looked back in front of me and froze. There was a little girl squatting in front of me. Her red-ginger hair was frizzy, sticking up in all directions, and freckles peppered her small face. Her tongue flicked out to brush her lips, revealing a missing front tooth as she grinned.

"The fishies weren't so bad," I heard myself say. I was relaxed now, no longer so panicked as when I'd fallen asleep. I even knew I was asleep but the knowledge did not seem so important in this place. "It was the shark I was worried about." The girl giggled and fell on her back, stretching her arms and legs like a star.

"Want to see the future?" she asked dreamily. Time seemed to slow and I fell flat on my back also, staring up at the sky, until I suddenly remembered the girl had asked me a question. I looked back at her but instead of a little girl, a large gray bear lounged in the sun. In my dream, this didn't surprise me.

"That's okay, I'm not so interested in the future," I said. The girl's voice whined but I spoke over her protests, "I'd rather see what happens for myself. There's no point if I already know what's going to happen." The girl who was now a bear listened to this information as I rested. The sun felt good on my face. When was the last time I'd lounged in the sun like this? Roc was never this warm...

"But you can change it," she said earnestly. "I think you'd want to change it, if you knew what was coming."

I didn't open my eyes but I grinned. "You're probably right, but then what would I have to complain about all the time? Thank you for your concern, but I'd rather not think about it."

The bear had turned back into a girl. She hovered over my head and I felt her breath on my face. I didn't stop smiling despite her obvious attempts to intimidate me. I knew she was angry for refusing her but I couldn't help feeling relaxed.

"No wonder she likes you so much," the girl said enviously. I opened one eye but she was gone. I sat up but knew already that I was alone again. Who liked me, I wondered. The thought drifted away like so many others and I eventually forgot it. The dream faded gradually although I continued to feel the warmth of the sun on my face. It was nice. It was comforting.

When I closed my eyes and opened them again, I was fully awake in my bed. I could hear the two guards Geoffrey and Carlyle talking to an older female voice. It was a comfortable speech with the occasional snicker. They didn't realize I was awake yet. The dream had faded at this point and I became more aware of my surroundings. The sun was peaking through my window softly, which meant that morning had arrived. People were probably awake now, I reflected, although not everyone. It would be easier to find answers now. I sat up and rubbed the sleep from my eyes, yawning softly. My companions abruptly stopped talking when they heard me.

"Go ahead and keep talking if you like," I said, feeling more refreshed and happy than I had in a long time. I felt ready for anything, even a round of questioning and some possibly uncomfortable punishments for being gone for so long. If everyone in the castle found out I'd gotten lost (for however long I'd been away) because of my own stupidity, I could only imagine the ways they would punish me. They wouldn't necessarily chain me in the dungeon, but I could sense the cold shoulders and the dirty looks I might get. Despite this, I felt prepared to deal with anything that came my way. After all, I wasn't in the lake anymore. That alone was worth anything that happened now. But first, I would get to know my new guards.

The terrified one from before, Carlyle, made a soft choking sound before Geoffrey, the braver one who'd helped me get to bed, elbowed him. The woman with them stared at me wide-eyed. Her blonde hair was tied back in a loose bun and her nose had a healthy splattering of freckles. She had a tray in her hands with two porcelain cups of what smelled like tea and a plate of cookies. I hopped out of bed, stretching appreciatively. I grinned again and approached the three of them, careful not to look too eagerly at the cookies. It felt like forever since the last time I'd eaten anything.

The woman, probably aware that I was looking at her (at the cookies), squeaked and hid behind Geoffrey. Carlyle took a visible step back and touched the hilt of his sword again, as he had the other night. I paused and my smile faded.

"What is it?" I asked, dreading the answer. I felt like my face must have melted off by the way they were staring at me. I forged ahead though, determined that my newfound braver would not disappear so quickly. "Why are you looking at me like that?"

"You honestly don't know?" Geoffrey asked as he was the first of his companions to compose himself. Did I really look that awful? "It's just that... you look... you resemble... the statue of King Christopher. You're him, aren't you?" Geoffrey said. He took a careful step toward me, as if he was frightened I would bite him.

"I don't know about any statue, but I am King Christopher. This is my room," I motioned to my bed and the windows, "and this is my castle. Have I really been gone so long that my own servants can't recognize me?" This was alright, I reminded myself. So I'd been a little off with the time. It didn't make a difference. So long as I maintained my calm, I could deal with anything that came at me. This was just... a minor setback.

"If he's a ghost, he'll get mad at you!" the woman stage whispered when Geoffrey began to argue. She watched me from behind Carlyle, her face pinched with fear. "Don't say anything to upset him. He'll do something terrible to us," she warned. "Ghosts know all manner of curses and spells from beyond the grave. You don't want to know what he could do to us!"

"Ghosts don't do bad things for no reason," Geoffrey said with a hint of irritation.

"But they can," Carlyle whispered. "They can curse you, I swear on my grand dame's grave, that's what I heard!" He held up one hand in a symbol of honor. The woman nodded vehemently, carefully moving her tray of tea to block her from me. I regretfully looked away from the cookies, knowing now that she'd probably see it as some sort of threat. Geoffrey sighed tiredly at his companions' behavior.

"That's witches, you ninny! Stop being so superstitious about everything. If he'd wanted to hurt us, he would have done it the other night. Anyway, he doesn't look like he can curse us," Geoffrey said, rolling his eyes. "He couldn't even get out of his own clothing!"

"H-Hey!" I protested. There wasn't any need for insults! Not that it mattered what I thought as they ignored me.

"Ghosts aren't supposed to look like they can curse you," the woman said with an air of knowing of such things, "but then wham! Your first born child comes out of your girl with goat horns and a tail. I swear it, I saw a girl that happened to. I can introduce you to her and she can prove I'm not lying."

"I'm not a ghost," I said, feeling strange that I even had to argue this particular point. I even touched the wall to prove that my hand didn't go through anything. They ignored me and continued bickering.

"That never happened, with a child being born like that, and you know it," Geoffrey said. He looked even more annoyed that she had some "proof" to offer him. "Martha was just saying all of that to get back at her husband for sleeping with the baker's daughter. She didn't actually mean her child was cursed or anything. Besides, I touched him before. My hand didn't go through him or nothing, as solid as you and me. If he was a ghost, that wouldn't have happened. I've seen it, how your hand goes through a ghost. He's not a ghost." The woman looked doubtful about the "you and me" part. Obviously, she did not have an affinity for the otherworldly crowd.

"He isn't going to curse us," Geoffrey insisted.

"Well, maybe he isn't a ghost," the woman conceded at last. She shifted the tea tray to one hip and rubbed her nose with her free hand. "But that just means he's probably a zombie."

Oh boy, I thought to myself.

"He'll want to eat us before long," Carlyle said in a horrified whisper.

"That's the dumbest thing I've ever heard you say," Geoffrey said, wide-eyed. The thought of my being a zombie obviously hadn't occurred to him. He scrambled to find a logical response.

"I'm not a zombie," I said. I wasn't even sure what a zombie would look like. Naturally I'd heard of them but... well, I wasn't one. Was I? No... I wasn't.

They continued to ignore me so I gave up trying to reason with them at all. As they argued over the chances of me deciding that one of them looked tasty enough to nibble on and debating over who should sacrifice him or herself so that the others might survive, I went into my closet to change into something more appropriate for a day among the breathing. The fact that I had stopped breathing at one point made me rethink the zombie thing, but the strangest thing was that I didn't feel dead. In fact, I felt better than I ever had before. I didn't think this information, however, would add to the conversation so I stayed quiet about it.

When I tried to tell them I was leaving, they didn't hear me, talking about how cutting off my feet would probably be a good way to make sure I couldn't chase them. Also, Carlyle argued, I might get distracted and eat my severed appendages.

Remembering just how unappetizing my feet must look after soaking in water for an indeterminate amount of time, I walked out the door and down the steps. It was obvious some weeks, maybe even months, had passed since I'd been away but I couldn't pinpoint just how much time that could have been.

Tact, I decided, would be my strategy for finding out what the hell had happened while I'd been away. That meant I wouldn't be waltzing in the front door or into the more popular rooms any time soon, much as I wanted to. My gut reaction was to turn the castle upside down and demand people tell me what was going on, but I'd learned already that tearing off impulsively was very, very stupid. Just look at the Widow's Lake debacle. I'd be taking things slow from now on, if only to stay "alive" (if that was the appropriate term) longer.

I snuck back into the kitchen and stole some rolls from the bread basket, munching on my stolen treats as I made my way out towards the main staircase. Strangely enough, I didn't make if two steps out of the kitchen before something strange happened.

After the first bite of a tasty-looking roll, I realized that not only had I lost my appetite but also that the normally delicious rolls tasted strange. It tasted like ash in my mouth and I couldn't even chew, the sensation was so disgusting. After I spit my mouthful into a rubbish bin, I left the remaining rolls on the table, feeling a bit uncomfortable with the single bite I'd taken. It was the strangest thing that had happened to me since I'd arrived at the castle. It also shook my good mood, depressing me a little.

To distract myself from the food (I'd never had a problem with the kitchen food before), I focused on my current predicament – what the hell was going on? The obvious solution awaited me in the library where I could ask Edward, the head librarian and historian in charge of writing down my family's long history. My most important questions were: how long had I been gone from the castle and what events had transpired in my absence? I was proud of myself for thinking of Edward so quickly: the tall, spindly old bookworm who hissed at everyone who entered his sanctuary of moldy books.

I grinned, remembering how the old grump loved me. He even let me drink the tea my maids brought especially for me, even while I read the adventure books in the library. It was our little secret that the smudges and wet spots on the pirate books were my fault. I was the only one allowed to do something like this – eat and drink while reading a book in the library. Father had been insanely jealous of the power I seemed to have over Edward and he was especially infuriated when he couldn't smoke his pipe anywhere near the library, even if he wasn't reading anything.

These memories of my childhood made me smile as I climbed up the stairs and walked down a wide corridor lined with bookshelves on either wall leading towards the library. When I was younger, I'd thought it was extremely clever to mark the passage to the library with books, specifically travel books with maps in them. Unfortunately, I seemed to be the only one who appreciated the irony of the design. Edward had thrown a fit, saying that putting the books there was a waste since no one would read them. Mother insisted that it was a wonderful touch of sophistication, since she had been the one who'd designed the corridor. So the books remained and Edward had to grind his teeth in fury. This tension was eventually diffused when the library had duplicate copies made in order to placate Edward. I grinned, remembering how agitated he'd get if Mother ever came to the library. They tended to butt heads over even the smallest things.

As I was thinking about Mother and Edward, I heard a noise off to my left. I glanced in that direction. The sound confused me; wasn't I the only one in the corridor? It had been eerily silent in the entire castle up until this point and I had no idea why I'd even heard the sound. I didn't even remember what it was, once I started looking around. I approached the direction of the sound and realized that it was coming from my father's old study.

Feeling as though I were breaking a rule, I slid up beside the wall and peered through the crack in the door. There was some faint light from the wide windows but it was still too dark to see inside the study itself. With the light at my back and the darkness before me, I couldn't see anything at first, only the faint light from the lamps and candles inside. I strained my eyes peering inside, noticing some strange shapes I could identify, until I realized there was a small group of men seated around a large table. My father's desk seemed to have been removed or pushed up against the wall – I couldn't tell which. My curiosity with this new development made me stop thinking about the library and talking to Edward. I'd learned long ago from the servants that listening to other people's conversations was a great way of finding out the truth faster. This might be an even better idea than the library, I reflected as I congratulated myself.

I pushed away from the door and hurried across the corridor to the opposite wall, directly across from the study. I climbed up onto the bookcase, watching my footing as I went so that I didn't make too much noise, and gently lifted the candlestick on my left side. Balancing for a moment on the balls of my feet, I used my other hand to twist the handle as if it were a door handle. A piece of the bookcase just under me, ironically a section of books about hidden islands somewhere in the world, opened inward at knee level. I replaced the candlestick and hopped down, using my momentum to slip inside the passage before it could close, navigating by hand in the dark. The passage closed silently behind me and darkness fell all around me, something that didn't bother me in the least.

I'd discovered this particular spot by accident as a boy, sword fighting with one of the coats of armor. In an effort to make a flourishing final move on the defenseless piece of metal, I'd flung my arm back and speared the candle with the tip of my sword. In my haste to return the twisted candle back to its place before I was caught, I'd opened the passage. It was one of my favorite hiding spots, as it was bare and undecorated – there was no pretense about the passage. It was an escape route for the most desperate of people and not meant to showcase the luxury and grandeur of the castle.

I used my fingers now to direct me as I crawled carefully up from my crouched position and used the crevices along the wall to stand. Again using the tips of my fingers, I reached behind me and found the cracks in the stone to climb up and over the place where the corridor was, as this particular gap between the walls outlined the corridor within like a cylinder. It was not a steep wall, as the corridor was, but rather a curved ledge with many cracks for me to climb over.

I paused at the top, thinking how frightened the servants would have been if they'd walked under the corridor knowing I was right on top of them. I continued down the other side, closing my eyes to focus on the pressure on my feet to find the cracks. I slipped the last bit down and landed in a small space between the wall of my father's study and the corridor I'd just crawled on top of. I rested my hand against one of the foundation pillars, taking strength from my castle as I crept more carefully to the wall of my father's study.

In this spot, light from the study dipped in through various cracks, showing me stone pillars with cobwebs and spiders all around me. I ignored this discomfort and slipped closer to the study's wall, looking through the peephole, made obvious by the light. I held my breath, observing the men in the opposite room.

They didn't look particularly interesting upon first glance. Most of them looked around as if uncomfortable being in the room. The lights flickered ominously and some of the men twisted to speak to each other, moving just enough so that I could see their faces. Many of them had the same general gaunt appearance, especially the older ones, and their hands made soft scraping sounds as they touched the table they sat at. I let my eyes drift over the rest of the room, vaguely listening as they made polite small talk about the weather.

Someone had changed my father's study since his death, but this was even more drastically different than when I'd last seen it. His desk was not the only thing that had vanished from inside. The paintings that had graced the walls before were strangely absent, leaving a discoloration against the wood, and chairs of various sizes and colors were pushed up against a long table where the men sat. There were no drapes on the windows anymore but the thick glass was barred, something else that had never been there before. The fireplace also contained a box of parchment paper instead of the pile of logs that normally resided there. If I squinted enough, I could just make out that the parchment was crisp and new, folded into what looked like a quarto.

I leaned my forehead against the wall, focusing on the voices as they spoke. It was a hushed murmuring, as if the men were afraid of being overheard. I smirked to myself, taking unnecessary pleasure from spying on them. And why shouldn't I? I hadn't been here long but I already knew they didn't belong here anymore than I wanted to marry Evelyn.

"– and the wife has gone back to her mother. You wouldn't believe how hysterical she was, throwing all of our old arguments back in my face as if this was all somehow my fault. Now, I know what the other men think of this situation and just what they would do if they knew I'd let my wife leave the castle, but I couldn't do anything about it. I thought to put my foot down and make her stay, like Fredric did with his wife, but the children didn't want to stay either. I couldn't face them every day the way things are going," one of the men closest to me said to his companion. I focused on him, letting my eyes focus on him instead of the rest of the room. His long gray hair was tied in a neat ponytail and a gold ring flashed on his pinky finger when he moved. He sipped from a glass of red wine and leaned closer to his companion. "If truth be told, I can't stand this place either. The walls groan at night, as if someone is there watching me. I couldn't even make love to my wife, close to the end."

"That's nothing," his companion, a thin, angular man said with a soft chuckle, "my wife ran away with one of the servants and came running back to me when she said one of the ghosts had spied her with her new lover. Can you believe it? She was so terrified, she had to come running back to me because she'd been caught by a ghost! I couldn't do anything but laugh."

"I couldn't even imagine that," Pinky-Ring said with sympathy. "The ghost was returned to the library, I hope?" he asked as he fiddled with the ring on his finger. Ghost-Man chuckled nervously and looked around the room, probably to make sure no one else was listening to them.

"Of course," said Ghost-Man as he leaned back. When he turned his head back around I saw that he had a mustache, finely cropped along his upper lip, which made his face look longer. I frowned in imitation, shifting my weight to my other leg. It was getting a little uncomfortable in my hiding place and the men had not said anything of interest yet. I was tempted to jump out at them just to get some sort of reaction but I dared not make a sound. I remembered all too well the way Geoffrey and Carlyle had looked at me when I'd come into my room the other night, not the mention my oath not to do anything stupid and impulsive again after the Widow's Lake. Besides, these men were more likely to do me a great injury if I came near. Stealth seemed a better tactic. I squared my shoulders and waited.

"Gentleman," a voice said from the front of the room.

I shifted my gaze up towards the opposite door, one I recognized as leading to the throne room. Part of me wondered if the throne room was still there or if they'd changed it since I'd left.

I pressed my forehead against the wall again, squinting to see the door. It was farther away than Pinky-Ring and Ghost-Man so it was difficult to make out details. A new man walked through the far door and took his place at the head of the table, a move that made him nearly invisible to me from my spot. All the men at the table stood and waited for the new person to sit before they too sat again, a general hush falling over them.

"Welcome," said the man in a bold, booming voice. It sounded strangely familiar but I couldn't place it. I must have known it from somewhere but at the same time, I felt as if I'd been thrust into a world I'd never been a part of before. This meeting, for example, was so surreal for taking place in my father's study. I kept envisioning his desk and the meetings he'd have with the advisors. I tried to focus on the conversation instead of this disconcerting feeling.

"I call this meeting of the People's Republic of Roc to order. Let us begin," said the new man. If I craned my neck and looked carefully between two stocky men, I could see that he wore a simple brown cloak edged in fur. The rest of his clothes were also simple, but there was a touch of elegance to them that could only come from extremely expensive material. He was trying to look poor, I realized, but by using material that denied that same claim. I found myself judging him already, scowling as I watched.

"The first order of business," said a man to the right of New-Guy. I looked towards him but he merely handed a piece of parchment to New-Guy, slouching back into his seat.

"Thank you, Joseph," New-Guy said. "I see from our agenda that we have some unfinished business concerning the kitchen servants. There have been complaints about poisoned food and some scandalous gossip about the wives, specifically the wives of party members. What course of action is suggested in this case and, please, let us discuss new ideas. We all know how little our attempts at torture will impact these heathens."

There was soft murmuring among the men and then Joseph, the man who'd handed over the agenda, stood and cleared his throat. I got the sense that he was very tall but otherwise I could barely make him out through the other men.

"I have a new suggestion," Joseph said to New-Guy. "Some of the men have thought that we might find a way to bring the servants... all the servants, I mean, closer to our cause. We thought that perhaps we could pass out more literature about our cause. We know that some are inclined to join with us but many remember the old monarchy. They do not wish to know us because they are comfortable with their old ways. We must rid them of their silly superstitions about the ghost king, as you have told us all countless times, Rue." I half grinned, realizing "Rue" was the name of New-Guy. This made remembering him easier for me, as he'd started becoming "New-Guy." Now, if I asked questions about him, I had a name.

"That is certainly true," said the man named Rue. "So you suggest passing out more literature to the servants? Do you also suggest that we start educating them in other ways as well?"

"That, at the very least, may ensure that they understand us a little better. We are not, after all, their enemies but their greatest allies. We are their rescuers," Joseph said, as if reading from a book. I frowned and leaned back, rubbing a hand over my eyes and then quickly pressed my face against the wall again. The dust was getting to me. I had to make sure I wouldn't sneeze and give myself away.

"This is very true," Rue said, leaning over the table. "What else do you suggest?"

"I have a suggestion," said Pinky-Ring. All turned in his direction as he stood and cleared his throat. I shrank back a little, making sure none of them could see me staring in at them. What would I have done if I'd seen an eyeball in the wall? "If I may speak, I have something to say."

"Certainly, Harold. You may speak freely here," said Rue in a regal voice. As I mentally replaced "Pinky-Ring" with "Harold," I reflected on Rue's tone. I sensed that my dear Rue was faking his behavior, trying to sound more important somehow. This only added to my snobbish disinterest with his choice of clothing – his poor/rich wardrobe. Or maybe he just naturally sounded like that, all stuck up and puffy.

"Well," said Harold, crooking his pinky finger in what I took to be a nervous habit, "I was thinking that perhaps we should start inviting some of the key members of the castle servants to the meetings. We could maybe speak with some of those whose parents were linked to the ancient spy network the king once commanded. They know this area better than anyone else, better than all of us combined, so I think that they might be a valuable asset. We could give them a role in the government so that they feel they are a part of the decision-making process. It was what my father intended when he first joined the People's Republic, and both he and I spoke at length together before I came to this meeting tonight."

"I remember your father's wise words," Rue said thoughtfully.

"I do not see the point in this," Joseph said, bringing all the eyes back to him. "They are only servants and, as we have seen time and time again, completely loyal to the old monarchy. You know that the guards who watch over the king's old room are the children of some of our revolution's most powerful enemies. They were in charge of helping the nobility escape from the castle during our glorious rebirth. They cannot be trusted."

"If we cannot trust them, then how can they trust us?" demanded another man farther to the left and out of my line of vision. Other voices joined in, agreeing or disagreeing. Every time someone came up with a seemingly brilliant explanation for or against the topic, someone else had an equally poignant reason arguing for the opposite.

I scowled as I watched the room dissolve into anarchy. This was ridiculous! How were any of them going to get anything decided if they didn't have some person with authority at their head to make the final decision? I'd thought that Rue was in charge, as his position at the head of the table spoke volumes about his supposed authority over the other men, but he only sat back and participated when he felt he needed to, and often in favor of his own opinion. He did not once seem to think of the good of the group, instead focusing on a very obvious personal agenda. This was getting ridiculously boring and useless and I'd learned precious little of what I wanted to know. I kept getting hints but never straight answers.

Some of what they'd said was interesting and I worried a little about the kitchen servants that they'd been talking about, especially the bit about torture, but I saw no harm in leaving the old windbags to argue out whatever they were going to argue. I could sense the way things were going to go because they'd said themselves that this issue had been left unresolved before. They were going to continue to bicker for this or that point and, in the end, they'd agree to disagree and be left with absolutely nothing decided. This was the problem if a group full of men felt they had the right to decide things together and there was no direction to the discussion. There also didn't seem to be any urgency to their decisions. When important things needed to be done, they eventually got decided. If these men didn't have a time limit, they'd never stop talking about it.

I left my hiding spot, half disgusted by their useless banter, and crawled over the rounded ledge to the secret passage on the other side of the corridor. As I slipped out, cautiously looking both ways, I continued on my path to the library. My head buzzed with more questions than before and I was even more determined to find the answers to them.

I did not know until later that I'd been seen walking away down the hall.

Interlude
The Bill of Freedom

The People's Republic of Roc
Preamble

We, the united people of the kingdom of Roc, declare ourselves hereafter a free people with the rights accorded to men with the principles of freedom, strength, and unity in our hearts. We the free people direct our efforts in the pursuit of justice to all and the equality of all men without boundaries or borders due to the illusionary restrictions of social class or monetary wealth. We strive for liberty and truth for our fellow man.

- II -
The Safe Haven

My old idea of finding Edward came back to me as I walked away from my father's study, using another secret passage to reach the second floor. The main library was close to the secret passage so I made a quick deviation from my original destination, always careful to hide from any potential people.

I saw people only once and when I did, only briefly. In this particular secret passage, I was wedged on top of a narrow beam between the corridor wall and the foundation of the castle, looking from about five feet off the ground down at the corridor through a wooden mesh. A terrified-looking woman in a rich green dress dragged a suitcase in one hand and a child in the other. The boy, no more than four years old, ran to keep up with what I assume was his mother. The terrified woman looked around the corridor as if expecting something horrible to come tearing down the hallway towards her. When this terrifying thing didn't come, she murmured something to the boy and they rushed off down the corridor and around a corner. I assumed they were heading for the exit but I couldn't be sure. Perhaps this was the wife of one of the men I'd seen. What was so terrifying, I wondered, about the castle that people seemed to run for the exits? I couldn't say.

I focused on getting through the secret passage without breaking my neck or making too much noise, letting my gut feeling alert me to any possible danger. I crawled out from under the wooden panels beside the library doors, brushing myself off as I stood. There were cobwebs all over my pants and shoes. I rubbed a hand furiously over my hair, scowling at the dust that had collected there. I must have looked like a ghost, I thought morbidly. I looked around to make sure I was alone before I approached my destination.

The wide mahogany double doors were closed when I reached them. This was not unusual. When I tried to open the doors, they were locked. This was unusual. The library didn't even have a lock on the door... I frowned and rattled one of the doors a little but it wouldn't budge. I grunted exasperatedly.

"There you are," someone said behind me. There was a soft gasp immediately following this statement. "You look terrible! Where have you been?" I scowled at the doors and glanced behind me at the woman from my bedroom. Geoffrey and Carlyle caught up with her in moments, panting as if they'd been running. I looked from one to the other of them, waiting for them to say something.

"What are you doing here?" Geoffrey asked at last.

"Ghosts don't need a reason to go somewhere they're haunting," the woman said mysteriously. "I'm Cathleen, by the by," she nodded to me, "and this is Carlyle and Geoffrey." She motioned to each man in turn. "We thought you should know our names... you know, so you feel less like cursing us."

"We've ruled out your being a zombie," Carlyle said helpfully. I rolled my eyes and tried the library doors again in a vain attempt to escape the coming conversation.

"I'm not a zombie and I'm not a ghost. Why is the library door locked?" I asked.

"No, we ruled out the likelihood of him being a zombie," Cathleen said to Carlyle. She waved her hand dismissively when he tried to protest. "He could still be one for all we know. We can't be too hasty with these sorts of things. If we let our guard down, the next second he'll just be taking a chunk out of your hand!"

"By the Seventh God, he's not a zombie," Geoffrey groaned. "We just talked about this!"

"I thought we decided he wasn't a zombie," Carlyle said with a note of alarm in his voice. He edged farther from me, although I hadn't moved.

"He probably isn't a zombie," Cathleen allowed reluctantly.

"I AM NOT A ZOMBIE!!!" Oops. I hadn't meant to yell quite so loudly. Judging by the way they were cringing, I must have looked pretty terrifying. Part of the effect, I knew, had to be the state I was in. Being covered in grime and cobwebs did not add to my sincere appearance, I was sure. Cathleen in particular seemed to become very interested in her shoes. I took a deep, cleansing breath and smiled. "I am not a zombie. Let's talk about something else."

They looked at each other and carefully straightened. Carlyle cleared his throat and Cathleen readjusted her uniform. Geoffrey smoothed over his expression and watched me for my next move. Their discomfort made me feel guilty so I tried to look friendlier.

"Do any of you happen to know why the library doors are locked?" I asked. The three glanced at each other again.

"Why do you want to go into the library?" Geoffrey asked carefully.

"I want to look at the histories," I said. When they looked as if they were actually listening to me this time, I continued my explanation. "I know I've been gone for a while but I have no idea for how long or what happened while I was away. I think Edward should be able to help me. He's the head librarian." Geoffrey and Carlyle kept looking at each other meaningfully but it was Cathleen who spoke.

"There are ghosts in the library," she said softly. She glanced at the door as if expecting them to rip open. As if the action would somehow stop this from happening, she made the sign of protection. "There's more than one in there too. They're angry all the time, as I'm sure most ghosts are. It is probably very uncomfortable to be a ghost. I heard there's one ghost who makes sure the others don't go out and bother anyone."

"Yeah, I know him. He's okay," Geoffrey said. Carlyle stared at him. "What?" he hissed, turning a bit pink, "Edward is a nice ghost. He's never said a mean thing to me. He told me stories about when my mom was a servant here."

When he said ghost, the word took a few seconds to register in my mind. Edward. Ghost. Edward is a ghost. Edward is dead. Dead.

The others were looking at me strangely. That's when I realized I'd been speaking out loud. I organized my thoughts around the voice screaming in my head, forcing my composure back into place. "How long has he been a ghost?" I asked.

"Since the revolution," Cathleen said just before Geoffrey clamped a hand over her mouth.

"Shhh!" he hissed. "Do you want them to hear us? You know better than anyone how many spies they have around the castle," he said.

"The what?" I said, arching an eyebrow.

"But that was..." Carlyle turned to stare at me, new horror in his eyes. "How could you know the ghosts before they died if you're not a zombie? It's been a hundred years," he said. The number didn't mean anything to me. I kept thinking it, the number one hundred, then I tried to picture one hundred years, then I stopped trying. It meant too much, meant far more than I could fathom just then. One crisis at a time, I told myself. I took a deep breath.

"Is there any way I can speak to Edward," I said. I even sounded calm. "It's very important that I speak with him. I don't know anything about any revolution or... anything. He can tell me what I'm missing." Cathleen glanced nervously at the double doors but stayed where she was. I guess fear can be stronger than curiosity sometimes.

Carlyle was shaking his head quickly. "I can't go in there," he whispered hoarsely. "I don't want to. Please." He clutched Cathleen's arm as if she would disappear – his knuckles were white, as was the rest of him. Geoffrey smiled reassuringly and patted his friend's shoulder.

SKULL JUGGLER

"Don't worry, you don't have to. I'll go in with..." here he paused and looked at me curiously. For a moment, I didn't know what he was asking me, but then I figured it out.

"Christopher," I supplied. "You don't... ah, don't worry. Just call me Christopher."

"I'll go in with Christopher," Geoffrey said, "And I'll tell you everything that happens once we get back, okay?" Carlyle nodded and sagged in relief. It was good to see him relax – his tension had put me on edge and I hadn't even realized it. Cathleen still looked worried but Geoffrey pointedly ignored her and turned to me. I forced my shoulders to relax and moved towards the doors. Geoffrey pulled a large brass key from around his neck and handed it to me.

I took the key and stared at it for a moment, surprised by how old it looked. As I mentioned before, the library had never had a lock on it before. If the new key looked this old, how old was I... what did this mean for me... one hundred years...

Pushing these thoughts away again, I held my breath and pushed the key in, resisting the urge to rattle the doorknob again as I turned the knob. Some signal I didn't notice must have reached whoever was inside. The doors of the library opened soundlessly and without any pressure from my hand, revealing the first dark bookcases on either side of the door. Beyond my vision darkness clouded in and there was a hint of the first reflective hues of purple and magenta from the stained glass windows further in.

From this angle, everything looked much as I remembered it, but touches here and there made everything feel alien. The candles by the left wall were lit, as usual, and the candle flames flickered in unison as they were supposed to, but the white wax was dripping upward, pooling on the ceiling. All the books also appeared to be perfectly in order and normal but, as I drew closer, I saw that the titles were all upside-down. Edward would have never allowed such a mistake and it struck me even more than the candles.

The wax bothered me but, otherwise, the library looked exactly as I remembered it. The low ceiling touched the tops of the big-shouldered bookcases and the delicate stained glass windows by the left wall reflected the meager light well. As I looked around, I saw that the oak desks by the windows were exactly as they'd always been: covered in various brown and green books strewn about as if someone had just been reading and got up to get another book. That had often been the case when I was here last. The librarians were on constant alert, moving between books at speeds that made my head spin.

Edward was the head librarian and oversaw all information exchange and documentation in the kingdom including but not limited to: tax information, national spending, peace treaties, war documents, birth records, death records, guild information, and even the price of sugar abroad. He accomplished all of his work effortlessly and with great pride. He had a group of five librarians under him who shelved and organized all the books in the library, seemingly endless in their tireless organization and reorganization whenever a new book arrived. All of the librarians had their particular sections in which they were proficient, but my father had often assured me growing up that even the youngest of them had forgotten more about the world of knowledge than we could ever hope to learn in our lifetimes. Edward was the one in charge of them all and he'd ruled his small corner of the kingdom sagely and, although he didn't want to admit he had any weaknesses at all, had a soft spot for me that allowed me to get away with almost anything. I was counting on that right now.

As I looked around, I felt a chill creep up my spine. It wasn't so much the strangeness of the situation but rather the emptiness of the desks and the absolute silence. Although Edward barked at anyone who breathed too loudly, there was always a soft hum to the air, some quality of expectation on the verge of noise. Here, now, there was no such feeling. The air was dead with the silence and I felt uncomfortable trying to bridge my old idea of the library and this strange, dark place. Geoffrey moved up to my elbow and almost walked into me. I hadn't realized I'd stopped walking. He looked around, peering around my shoulder.

"Is there something there?" he said softly. He didn't so much whisper as breathe the words into my ear. I was tempted to speak softly as well.

"It's just not what I remember, is all," I said in my normal tone of voice. It felt too loud and I regretted speaking the second the words left my mouth, but they were said. The echoes faded once they had left their creepy presence, at which point the silence pressed in again.

"What do you remember?" Geoffrey mumbled. He tried speaking a little louder and stood straighter, determined not to let me out-macho him. I kept my expression blank, thankful for the sounds even if they felt awkward.

"I remember a lot more commotion," I said. My voice was steady and calm so I continued before I could chicken out again. "There were always people around to talk to me... and there was never any time that I was alone here. They watched me like a hawk."

"Sounds like you were a trouble-maker," Geoffrey said. I looked back at him and saw the corners of his mouth twitching.

"Are you making fun of me?" I asked, raising an eyebrow at him. "Not scared I'll eat your eyelids or something?"

"Nope," Geoffrey said confidently, breaking into a full grin. "If you wanted to do that, you would have gone for Cathleen. She's got much tastier-looking eyelids then I do."

I couldn't help but laugh, shaking my head. Geoffrey relaxed all at once, grinning at me. The smile didn't leave my face as I walked towards the next aisle, peering between books for any sign of life.

"Why is this place so empty?" I asked, feeling more comfortable now that Geoffrey didn't think I was going to eat him. "I thought you mentioned something about ghosts? As much as I'd love to see one, I'm starting to think you were just pulling my leg." Geoffrey moved away from me down another aisle, reaching towards one of the books. He trailed his finger on the spine of one and drew his finger back, almost black with dust.

"You have to be careful around here," Geoffrey said, wrinkling his nose. "Things feel differently than you expect them to."

"Hmm," I said, looking at the brass numbers at the top of the bookcases. Each one sparkled dimly in the candlelight and the stained glass windows shifted the light to add an even gloomier effect. Geoffrey and I drifted through the library, touching things here and there, mostly to remind ourselves that it was all real. With the strange lighting and the candle wax drifting to the ceiling, it was easy to forget what reality was. As we passed the travel section with various maps nailed to the bookcases, we neared the more historical books. They were particularly disorderly and half hanging out of their shelves.

"It doesn't seem the ghosts are around right now," Geoffrey said, perhaps remembering my comment from before, as he traced the spine of a faded red book, pressing it back into place.

"Do not touch that, please," a firm voice said. A head materialized under Geoffrey's fingers with a disapproving expression on his face. Geoffrey leapt back into a chair and nearly fell over into another bookcase, ducking behind me as quickly as he could. I tensed and backed up until we were pressed against one of the windows, bathing us in purple and blue light. The rest of the figure materialized and came towards us, wringing his hands as he came.

"I do apologize for the fright I must have given you, but I must insist that you do not touch that book, please. I am the head librarian here and it is my duty to dissuade you from touching the royal family's property. As the royal family no longer draws breath, may the Seventh God preserve them, it falls to me to protect their valuables. Only the-," he stopped speaking when he noticed me. His eyes widened and he sucked in his breath through his teeth. "Gods save me... are you a ghost?"

Geoffrey made a strangled sound and waited for me to speak. I drew a blank, staring at the figure instead of speaking. He had asked the question as if ghosts couldn't possibly exist and I was something remarkable – ironic since he was still partially inside the bookcase. Geoffrey elbowed me sharply in the back and shoved me forward.

"Well... I don't think I'm a ghost," I said, rubbing my spine. "Why can't he touch the book? This is a library, isn't it?" I took in details now: the wringing hands, the carefully groomed appearance of the ghost, the shiny brass buttons on his jacket and the nearly transparent shoes that came in and out of existence as the ghost approached us. The signs pointed to Edward and he had said he was the head librarian, but my mind couldn't process this anymore than it could absorb the transformation of the library. It was too bizarre to soak in. Edward was the kind of person so steeped in reality and facts – seeing him as a ghost seemed like the worst cosmic joke anyone could think of.

"You must be a ghost," Edward said earnestly. "You have been gone so long, Your Majesty. Please, let me ring for some sandwiches and tea. You must tell me all about your journey, for the books," Edward floated forward (he was indeed floating) and passed right through the chair Geoffrey had tripped over. The ghost, Edward, deftly pulled the offending book from the bookcase with the practiced ease of someone who always had done this, and tenderly ran a hand over the front cover. I recognized it, now that it was out, as the historical records book where every recorded testimony of my immediate family was stored, although it looked so old and worn that I'd have sworn that I'd never laid eyes on it before.

I didn't feel at all frightened anymore. I'd known Edward for my entire life and he probably knew me better than anyone else in the world. For some reason, I didn't think being dead changed much. He still petted books as if they were alive, he still wrung his hands, as if he wasn't accustomed to having them empty, and he still worried that I didn't eat enough (if I was a ghost, why would he worry about my being hungry anyway?). None of that had changed. None of the important things about Edward had changed.

"Edward, how am I supposed to say this?" I murmured. "Don't you know you're de-,"

"Shhh!" he whispered quickly. For a moment, the lights flickered and the walls shook. Geoffrey grunted and clung to the bookcase, dislodging several books to the floor before everything stilled. Edward looked around fearfully and hurried to return the disturbed books to their proper place.

"Don't say it," he whispered even more softly. "I know what I am, but the others are not at all pleased with the current arrangements. Everything was a bit more manageable before the exterminator came to the castle and gave the boot to the ladies from the guest rooms, but the Queen has been utterly intolerable since the beginning." He bowed his head. "Have they found you somewhere in the castle and forced you here, like us? That will not do at all. The King should never be forced here, with all of... in the present situation, it would be grossly inappropriate and..." Edward stopped speaking at this point. His hands shook as he removed his spectacles and cleaned them with a handkerchief from a pocket, the same handkerchief my father had given Edward upon making him the head librarian. I felt strange seeing it, that little touch of my reality peeking back at me, and almost missed what he said next.

"Your Majesty," he said, "it is just so good to see you again. A friendly face after the dismal existence I have been subjected to, although I confess that this trial is indeed a trial against my loyalty and my sense of duty to the crown. Sire, I have done the best that my abilities have allowed, without complaint or disrespect to those under my charge, although I confess to my pain now in my current circumstance. And although I am glad you are here, if you are indeed a phantasm as I have suggested you may be, I wish that you were absent from this place."

When he'd said his peace, Edward began to cry. Geoffrey reached out to pat his shoulder but his hand went through him, as if Edward was made of smoke. Geoffrey shuffled next to me, unsure what to do now that the big scary ghost had started to cry.

"Edward," I said, "I'm sorry for the pain you have suffered during my absence. To be perfectly honest, I have no idea what I am, a ghost or what. I feel alive and whole, I can and do touch anything solid, but I don't understand how I could have been missing for one hundred years without aging or changing. I felt myself die... but I'm not dead. At least, I'm not entirely dead. I don't understand it anymore then you do."

Edward stifled his crying and dabbed at the corner of his eyes with the handkerchief, taking a deep breath to calm down.

"Where were you, Sire?" he asked. "We searched for you, everyone did, every where we could think of to search. The guards were frantic to discover your whereabouts; even the maids helped in the search. Some of the braver ones searched the cellars and the wine rooms, even though you detest the cellars. Where were you all of this time?"

"I was in the Widow's Lake," I said.

Edward's eyes widened. "You were inside the Widow's Lake? But I could have sworn... wasn't it only a legend?" He wrung his hands, looking about wearily. Geoffrey was staring at me now too, I could feel his eyes burning into my back, but I refused to look at me.

"I remember drowning," I explained. "I remember being trapped there for a long time, and I remember my escape. I had help from the Skull Juggler."

"The what?" Edward said blankly.

"Don't you remember the Skull Juggler from my father's death festivities? It was him, I think. He wasn't wearing his mask but... I'm fairly certain it was him," I said. Edward's eyes narrowed to slits and he pursed his lips until they turned even whiter than they already were. I noticed at about this time that he was progressively floating higher off the ground, either because of his agitation or because he didn't seem bothered by gravity anymore. This strange phenomenon reminded me of where I was, what was really going on. I'd started to forget that this wasn't just another normal conversation with Edward on a rainy day.

"I did not consider that the Skull Juggler could have had such a heavy hand in the present situation," Edward said. "This man saved you from the lake? He is still alive after all this time, enough that you recognized him when you saw him again? He must be a true Deathwaker, as we feared. Where is he now?"

"I have no idea where he is now. He hasn't changed since the day I saw him last and he acted like he knew everything that's happened to me since the party one hundred years ago." My thoughts jumped to the conclusion I saw forming on Edward's face. "You think that he had something to do with my being in the lake in the first place."

"You do not sound surprised about my suspicions," Edward observed.

"I've thought about it before," I said. "I wouldn't put it past him to do it but I don't know how useful that knowledge is right now. The time has passed and I am here now. I am dead. And I don't think I can do anything to change that at present. I want to do what I can to help right now. So what can I do?"

"Nothing, I expect," Geoffrey said. Edward glanced at him as if he just remembered the still-breathing guy was still there. Funny, I just realized that Geoffrey was the only living one in the library. Edward and I, I realized with some amusement, were dead. No wonder Geoffrey looked so pale. "Well," Geoffrey started when he realized we were staring at him, "well, they're ghosts. All the people here are ghosts. What can you do if they're already dead?"

"I'm not sure," I admitted. Something occurred to me then, as I looked around the room. "Did you say there are more of you in here?"

Edward nodded gravely. "All those who... are no longer substantial now reside within the safety of my walls," he said. "At first, meaning right after we all came to the library after we'd died, we could all intelligently discuss the metaphysics of being ghosts and being, in a sense, conscious again of our own existence. Soon, though, people became extremely touchy about the subject. We can say the word "ghost" or "phantasm" here but actually saying the D-E-A-D word makes people very uncomfortable. The others have found various places to reside, so they generally stay out of my way. Some of the ladies have migrated to the wash room and the men have mostly clustered around the adventure section." I nodded thoughtfully.

"If you wrote down everything that happened," I said to Edward, "it might be possible for us to piece together what exactly happened. I have information that you lack... but you also know a great deal more about what's happened at the castle than I do. I've only had bits and pieces, and all filtered in questionable forms."

"There is much I can tell you," Edward said eagerly, "if you allow me to record your version of the events, I can fill in the gaps in your knowledge so that you understand what happened."

"Good. Is there a room where we can speak in private?

If you wish to record what I've been through, I don't want people coming in and out trying to scare Geoffrey," I said. Geoffrey glared at my insult to his masculinity but didn't deny it either. Geoffrey, I reflected, was not an idiot.

"You would do that for me?" Edward said breathlessly. "Sire, it is an honor to record your family's history. I would very much enjoy taking down the details of your experience in the Widow's Lake and all the other interesting things you may have done since you were gone."

"Certainly, Edward," I said. I put a hand carefully on Geoffrey's arm. He didn't jump this time, a surprise after the way he'd been treating the whole "dead" situation up until that point, and I smiled. Despite everything that had happened, I still wanted to be liked. I didn't realize until that moment how much his aversion towards me had bothered me. "If you need me, just come get me. This shouldn't take too long," I said.

"Okay, I think that should be fine. I'll wait for you to finish," he said. He glanced at Edward carefully and coughed into his hand, turning a bit pink. "Edward is the only nice ghost here. You should let him do as he likes. It's only right." With another nervous glance at Edward, he headed for the large double doors. He paused long enough to see if anyone was still outside waiting for him and then slipped out.

"That boy has grown so quickly," Edward said. He removed the handkerchief from his pocket and patted his temple gently. "His mother was such a good woman, may the Seventh God rest her soul. You do know who she was, don't you?"

I shook my head. "No, I have no idea. Should I?" I said.

"The cook, the woman you seemed so close with. Her name was Abigail... she became the head cook after Maggie left, long before all this mischief transpired," Edward said.

Images of Abigail filled my mind: her white uniform stained with tomato and pepper sauce, her quick hands lifting heavy pots steaming with delicious smells, her shy smile when I came near enough to steal a freshly-made muffin, the way she hummed in the evening after a long day's work, her infectious love for all the servants in the kitchen, even when they teased her. And the next moment I saw my father's cold, reeking corpse on the marble dais during his funeral, the way his eyes were stuck wide open and full of pain, the hundreds of flowers all around trying to keep the stench from making everyone sick. My mind tried to force these two images together and couldn't. I ran a hand over my eyes and huffed sharply, forcing myself to stop thinking about it. I couldn't, I just couldn't think about it.

"He doesn't look a thing like her," I mumbled.

"Indeed," Edward said as he nodded. He led me deeper into the library towards his personal office where all of the oldest and most fragile books were kept under lock and key. Edward drifted through the door and clicked the lock so that I could follow. I did so, carefully holding my rampaging thoughts at bay.

Interlude

The Book of Horn by: Jacob Fire

Chapter 11 "Zombies"

Introduction

The word for an animated corpse, "zombie," has been one of the biggest mental obstacles for fledgling necromancers since the beginning of time. One of the largest misconceptions that the living have about us is that we as necromancers are nothing more than intelligent (and often evil) zombies. The differences between necromancers and zombies are enormous.

To begin, refer to Chapter 6 "The Act" and note that one of the requirements to become a necromancer is the retention of the soul. Another requirement is the predisposition towards magic, which manifests after The Act. These two requirements (the possession of a soul as well as the potential for magic) are completely absent from a zombie. This chapter will go more in-depth on this subject, as it is one all necromancers should be aware of even if they do not use zombies in their usual work.

What is a Zombie?

As a general definition, a zombie is described as a moving or "animated" corpse that obeys the commands of the necromancer who raised it. A zombie is only the shell of a living creature and holds neither a soul nor a mind. They cannot speak, eat, sleep, love, or think in any way. As an example, think of a puppet. When the puppet is left alone, it simply lies on the floor. The necromancer is the puppeteer, often skilled but not always. Even an unskilled necromancer can raise a zombie – a dangerous experiment to perform without the supervision of a senior.

To Make a Zombie

One notable reason the living fear us is our callous treatment of dead bodies. Since we are dead ourselves, over time we are no longer bothered by graveyards or other burial areas and we tend to enter without the same sense of reverence as other people do. In order to create a zombie, you must first acquire a body. This can be done in a number of ways and with different types, but the best results come from the freshest bodies (hanged victims are often the best as their bodies are discarded the fastest). DO NOT attempt to create a zombie from cremated remains – the body is too disorganized (and usually mixed with other ingredients) to be used properly. Search for a newly dead corpse and always under the supervision of your senior.

Once you have a body, locate something that holds a memory of the being to who the body once belonged. This can be any object that belonged or came into contact with the body in question. From there, your senior will walk you through his or her personal method of zombie-raising, as the method is unique to specific factions. Again, do not attempt to raise a zombie without the aid of your senior.

As a side note, note that raising zombies is not limited to raising the bodies of people. Animal bodies can be just as useful.

Maintenance

Be prepared to discard your zombie as soon as you are able. The living will easily smell the decaying flesh and there is often the danger of the body falling apart all on its own, usually during the most crucial times that you need it most.

Some tips – seek an earth necromancer's potions to shield the smell, keep the body away from the elements as much as possible, and avoid graveyards, as they tend to remind the zombie of where it would rather be. Discard the zombie properly as soon as you have finished with it.

Discarding Zombies

Do not leave your zombies anywhere that they might negatively impact a living population. This includes leaving the body in a drinking well or in a plague-infested area. Try to bury the body if you can or leave it somewhere that is easily accessible to scavengers. This will make things simpler for all involved.

Zombies can be useful helpers when used appropriately. Consult your senior with more specific questions about zombies. Past the general information, zombie-raising is faction-specific. For more detailed information on zombie theory, famous zombies in history, and the uses for a zombie, refer to the Table of Contents or the glossary at the end of this book.

- 12 -
Memories

Edward's private study was full of even more dust and cobwebs than the secret passages I'd been crawling through all day, with little spiders skirting the desk in a vain attempt to escape Edward as he hissed at them. Edward drifted towards the single bookcase on the opposite wall and wrung his hands as he searched the top shelf for something I couldn't see. I went to the moldy green armchair by the fireplace and smacked it a few times to clear at least the superficial dust. I coughed and slapped my hands together to clean them and sat down, feeling the dirt all over my body even as I made an effort not to touch the chair with my bare skin.

Edward drifted back to me with a small carrying case in his left hand and the red book in the other. He placed the materials on the lectern by the desk and opened the case, removing inkpots, quills, spare scraps of paper, some knives to sharpen the quills, and a small round stone. I peered closer and froze when I realized what it was. I'd seen it a few times before and, looking at it now, I remembered very clearly what it was.

Edward had once had a wife, long before I was born. She and their son had died in one of the many plagues, in a distant land, in a time I'd never known. It was all very mystical when I'd been growing up, something mysterious that only made me like Edward more, so mysterious that I shadowed him persistently. Marianne, one of the friendlier cooks, was the one who'd told me the truth about the stone: it was a piece from his wife's gravestone.

I'd only seen it once or twice before, and only when I snuck in and hid somewhere to spy on the librarians. Marianne only told me what it was because she knew that I was planning to steal it and play with it, something so childish and stupid that I thought I'd never stop feeling ashamed about it. I remembered how she'd comforted me as I cried about what a horrible little brat I was. I also remembered how she'd given me some cake to cheer me up. I even remember how surprised Edward looked when I gave him the cake instead, crying and miserable. I was a pathetic child.

Now she was dead. Now he was dead. I could smell my father's corpse, the memories were so firmly ingrained in my mind.

I forced away the image and focused on Edward as he assembled his materials, occasionally reaching out to stroke the stone between movements. It seemed like the most real object in the room, glowing faintly in the dim light. Did Edward think about his wife in death? Did she come to visit him? How could he touch the physical tools when he wasn't real anymore? How could he touch the book if he was a ghost? Was his wife a ghost too? If she wasn't a ghost, then what was she? Where was she? Questions swirled in my head, a relief from the morbid images I'd been thinking of before. At last

Edward opened the book to a particular passage and dragged his finger slowly down the text, his eyes following. I waited as patiently as I could, leaning away from the moldy seat.

"Edward... where are the other librarians? Are they... ghosts too?" I asked, still consumed by my questions about ghosts. If I could understand what ghosts were, maybe I could understand what the hell I was.

Edward drew in a sharp breath and curled his fingers tightly around the lectern. "I don't know. I never found out what happened to them," he said. He cleared his throat and wiped his chin with the handkerchief from his pocket. It was a nervous gesture he could never hide.

"We don't know much of what happened that night," Edward began in his storyteller voice, obviously determined to change the subject, "since there was such a great deal of pandemonium, but here is what we have evidence of. The last time anyone saw you in the party itself was directly before the fire-breathers. I am sorry to tell you that they were the first victims accused of your death and they were executed soon after your disappearance was confirmed. Going back to that night, the next time anyone saw you, you were in the gardens, where you quickly departed, according to the young lady witnesses. Is there any particular reason you left so abruptly, Sire?" Edward paused to scrutinize me.

"The young ladies you are referring to were trying to catch me in a romantic mood," I said with a sigh. "The whole reason I left the ballroom was to escape becoming the next attempt at an arranged marriage. The garden was worse than I had expected, so I didn't stay."

"Understandable," Edward said as he carefully wrote notes on the side of his larger narrative. The words appeared milky-white on the page and then solidified into black. Whatever he was doing, Edward was concentrating enough that his pen was leaving a physical imprint on something he should not have been able to change. I knew that it was his familiarity with the book and all of his previous writings that kept Edward tied to this world and this moment was one that he would have given anything to experience, either alive or dead. When he finished writing some notes, he pressed his finger lightly to the page and found his place in the narrative again.

"During this interval, the fire-eaters finished their performance and the Lady Raquel of Duhn made a speech. She spoke very eloquently, I am told. One of my scribes reprinted her speech here:

"Welcome honored guests. Many of you already know who I am, but for those of you who do not, allow me to introduce myself. I am the Lady Raquel, daughter of the Lord and Lady of the House of Duhn, good friends of the Charnel family — and thus dear friends of the darling birthday girl. It is my esteemed privilege and honor to welcome you to our dear Lady Evelyn's fifteenth birthday celebration. We have been waiting for this year for a long time. This is an age of change, an age of growth. When the sun has crossed the heavens long enough to watch such as she grow into such a lovely young woman, one can only hope that one can spend just a little time basking in her presence. That is the kind of person Evelyn is, one who brings us all together under the canopy of friendship and courtly courtesy.

"Evelyn has officially come out to society now for an entire year and soon she will announce her most recent engagement. Do not be angry with me, Evelyn, I simply could not contain my joy for you any longer. Yes, honored guests. It falls to me to announce Evelyn's secret marriage engagement, although I will keep the identity of the lucky gentleman a secret for Evelyn to reveal herself, when she is ready. Oh, she only looks angry but she is actually quite pleased. I know she has wanted to reveal the truth for some time now. This only goes to show the depth of character and commitment to friends that Evelyn holds so dear, and why so many of you have come to Roc in order to celebrate her special birthday.

"I would also like to commend her charming cousin, His Majesty the King of Roc, for hosting such a splendid event in his dark, exotic, and beautiful country. Where is the scoundrel? No... not anywhere that I can see. No doubt we shall see him soon. This is, after all, his party! So please, raise your glasses with me, to Evelyn. Happy birthday, my dear friend.

Edward paused and looked up at me. "I am told that the Lady Evelyn privately forbade her from ever returning to Roc after she gave this speech."

I chuckled. "The Lady Raquel is a menace," I said. "She is a singularly unpleasant creature to associate with. I didn't much care for her but I am surprised Evelyn allowed her to give a speech in her honor at all."

"Sire, about the wedding she was talking about..." Edward said hesitantly.

"Mother was determined that I would marry Evelyn," I said.

"I knew it!" Edward said. I raised my eyebrows at his

excitement. "There was a great deal of speculation over this issue, Sire," Edward explained. "I and several others believed that you were the man expected to marry her, especially because she did not marry anyone after your disappearance, although there were some other wild guesses. Some seemed plausible but I always knew that it had to be you."

"Well, now you know," I said, feeling a tad annoyed. Of all the things to worry about, why was everyone always so interested in stupid things like that? "I spoke with Armand the day I disappeared. According to him, Mother was attacked by assassins and nearly killed. She was forced into accepting my Uncle Albert's offer of protection, in exchange for my marriage to Evelyn." Edward's eyes rounded at my words and as he scribbled feverishly in the book, I spoke in more detail about what I knew.

"It is all... very amazing," Edward said. "How all of these coincidences occurred so close together, and so suddenly. All of these events seem to have stemmed directly from your father's death festivities and the Skull Juggler's performance."

"I know," I said glumly.

"Anyway..." Edward said, sensing my mood, "When the Lady Raquel mentioned your absence from the party, the Queen became aware of your disappearance, although she did not think it was so serious as it later became. She and Mathew, your personal advisor, they left the ballroom for a number of minutes before you vanished. When she returned, she sensed that your disappearance was atypical. She mentioned something about a rumor circulating about you and marriage. According to her own testimony..." Edward peered closer at the book, "she stated that you knew the consequences of leaving the party early and would not have done so under normal circumstances. In order to find you, she spoke in private with the servants and sent men to search for you, although she did not immediately announce her suspicions to her guests since she felt that discretion was necessary in this instance."

"That's Mother," I said sardonically, "always worried about discretion."

"Yes," Edward said, trying to hide a smile with a fake cough. He turned the page and added a quick note on the side of the book and then began reading again. "According to my timeline, the servants searched for close to an hour in all of the usual locations – your room, the kitchens, some of your favorite hiding places, such as your father's study – but they could find you nowhere. At this point, the Queen began to worry that something terrible had befallen you and sent for the captains of the guard. Again, she spoke to them in the utmost secrecy and demanded they search the entire castle and the grounds. The soldiers checked the cellars, the catacombs to your rooms, the attics, the servants' quarters, and finally, the stables.

"There they found a young servant boy who said he'd seen you," Edward continued. "The boy spoke of your great agitation and insisted you had been escaping demons or some other supernatural danger. He said that he could not see what you ran from but he offered to fight whatever it was for you. He tried to help the soldiers as much as possible, but they could not find you anywhere even with his help."

"What happened to him?" I asked, remembering how scared the boy had looked that night. My behavior, I reflected, must have looked very strange indeed to someone who had no idea what I'd been escaping from. I vaguely remembered the words I'd exchanged with him and it made sense, what he'd suspected.

"The boy left the castle several days after your disappearance," Edward said, adjusting his spectacles higher on his nose. "He was determined to find you again and bring you home. The only other fact I know is that his name was Roger Farre. I have never heard of him again since he departed, and I only know of his departure because one of the servants told me after all of us became ghosts." Edward leaned back, writing a quick note in the margins, and then looked back up at me. "May I continue?"

"Of course," I said. I thought again of my dead father and suppressed the image, focusing on Edward's words. None of it felt real, it was too much like listening to an entertaining story.

"At this point," Edward said, "the entire castle was aware of your disappearance. The guests who remained offered to aid the guards and, within a few minutes, a search party was formed to safely explore the forest. A lot of people were convinced that you were being held captive for ransom by traveling bandits. Others insisted that you were already dead." Edward paused, smiling at me sadly. I could practically hear what he was thinking: I never would have thought these people would be right!

"A few people even speculated that the Skull Juggler's work had finally been accomplished and you were now acting as his zombie, a walking corpse only half alive. The Queen quickly suppressed these public voices and continued searching for you. The real trouble began the next morning, when word of your disappearance spread outside of the castle walls. Servants can never keep quiet about what happens in the castle and such gossip as this could not be suppressed no matter how many punishments the queen promised. Wild and far-fetched speculation followed in accordance with your disappearance.

"A small but vocal group gathered later in the day at the public ale houses and began seriously discussing some of the conspiracy theories. This group decided that the best course of action they could take would be to destroy the fire-breathing sisters, as they'd been the entertainment. They decided that if the Queen had brought the Death-waker to your father's death festivities and now she had invited the fire-breathers, it must naturally have been their doing that you had disappeared. This mindset also assumed that you were already dead and beyond our assistance, which made martyring you easier. You have no idea the kind of panic the Death-waker caused when he came to Roc. The propaganda in the castle didn't extend to the lower classes and the servants had their own speculation that they were only too happy to spread."

"I can imagine," I said softly.

"The first order of business," Edward said, "for the People's Republic, as this group of mostly men was called, was a quiet investigation of the castle. They first tortured and killed the fire-breathers, though, to show that they were intensely serious in their motivations. There had been too much unexplained death of late to leave the peasants at ease. They felt that there must have been some sort of conspiracy from the beginning to kill the heirs to the throne. The People's Republic had a natural target in your mother, the Queen. They believed it was she who had killed your father, the King before you. They felt that the Queen was eliminating you from the line of succession so that she could begin a new family of her own bloodline with her choice of husband and child. It was because of this speculation that some radical members began to conspire to kill the Queen. Judging by the information you gave me just a few minutes ago, it sounds that they might have also been involved in your mother's near-assassination the night before your disappearance."

"You cannot be serious..." I whispered. I finally understood what it all meant, all of the craziness around the castle, how every room seemed eerie and empty, the terror of the servants, the strange question Geoffrey and Carlyle asked about seeing a statue of me somewhere. "They killed everyone," I said, finally understanding what that meant. Edward nodded slowly.

"They did, but not immediately. To destroy a monarchy requires a great deal of time and planning, not to mention a lot of servants had to be bribed and silenced before even the planning could take place. Unfortunately, during that time, the Queen did not make their argument for her supposed betrayal any weaker. Soon after your disappearance was considered permanent, she married your personal advisor, Mathew, and gave birth to a daughter exactly a year after you disappeared." Edward lifted his eyes from the book and waited for my reaction.

"She married… she had a… I have a sister?" I said, my eyes widening. It made sense, in a cold, distant sort of way. She was Queen. The bloodline must continue. She probably didn't even have a choice about having another husband and another child. She'd have rather kill herself than allow Uncle Albert or even the Voulders to take the throne instead. I intellectually understood this. The jealousy and anger I felt didn't understand that intellectual common sense.

"Her name was Anne," Edward said softly. "She was only a child, she didn't know what she would be involved in, nor what her birth would spark. It was the perfect opportunity for the rebels to take over. With so much of the staff occupied with the birth and all the planned celebrations that were to follow, the parade, the parties all over the country, all the guests planning to come, it was impossible to keep track of every little thing. They had no problem sneaking some spies in and eventually storming the castle at the perfect time. It was…" Edward stopped, taking a deep breath.

"They destroyed everything, killed everyone they could find. The servants who were bribed were barely safe from the zealous fighters. Even the betrayers were forced to use all their knowledge of hidden passages to escape their own slaughter. According to my records, many of the nobility living in the castle at the time were able to pay some of the castle's loyal servants to escape undetected. The Lady Evelyn and your newly born sister were able to escape the castle thanks to some of the maids and, as far as I know, they are still safe. I was able to use one of the secret passages through the library to get them out and I watched them reach the forest, but after that I don't know what happened to her."

"What happened to those who couldn't escape?" I asked, already knowing the answer. I suddenly thought of Richard and his family. Were they safe? But no, I didn't have the guts to ask Edward what had become of the Rannoch family. I felt safer not knowing.

"Different things..." Edward said. "Most of the servants who remained in the castle were killed outright and there are many horror stories about women who were raped and brutally murdered. The younger members of prominent royal houses were sometimes publically executed, as a message to neighboring countries to keep out, as much as a warning to the public. Those who survived immediate execution were tortured for information on any future rebellions against the People's Republic. The whole process was extremely bloody and very few prisoners escaped at all, except for the members of the wealthiest families with even wealthier foreign relatives, those family members who managed to pay the rebels outrageous ransoms for their hostages. None of the women captured survived."

I tried to absorb this information, tried to apply the image of my dead father to hundreds of people all at once, all people that I knew, and my mind went blank. I exhaled sharply and rubbed my forehead, staring at the wall to distract myself. There had been a painting there once but, staring at the spot now, I could see that there was something not right about the blank wall. It seemed as if the room missed the painting and strained for it. The whole room felt like that, like it was leaning into a single point, towards me.

"What happened to Mother?" I whispered. My voice came out so softly that I thought Edward hadn't heard me.

"She was brought to trial," Edward said. "The rebels accused her of a great deal of nonsense and then demanded to know what she had done with your dead body. When she ordered them all to go to hell, they decided that public execution was the only thing to be done with her. But... well, the viewing public could not stomach it, to watch their reigning Queen murdered before their very eyes. She was of the purest royal blood and your mother, the Martyr King as you were called for several years. The rebels were forced to change tact, and quickly. On the day of your mother's execution they brought her to the town square. She was already wearing a noose around her neck, something done more as a joke than as a threat. The peasants nearly had a revolt of their own that day. Instead of risking the wrath of those who'd initially been on their side, the members of the Public's Republic held a quiet beheading behind the stables where few ventured. Your mother was buried, with her head, in a place of honor in the royal cemetery, to keep people happy."

It didn't feel real. I stopped listening to Edward and leaned into my hands, pressing my palms into my eyes. The dull pain of the gesture helped clear my head a little and I tried to piece it all together. Mother was dead, Edward was dead, and probably everyone else I knew was dead. I had seen them all so recently it seemed but now they were simply gone. People I had taken for granted my entire life were just... gone. It blew my mind, thinking about it.

"The castle was burned down," Edward continued in a strained voice, as if he understood how I was feeling. "A tomb was constructed beside the still-smoldering ashes and thousands of people still visit it daily, offering their respects and prayers to you. They say that you were the Seventh God incarnate in human form. They say, even now, that you were Merciful to all." I snorted but didn't look up, keeping my eyes closed against my hands. "The highest ranking rebels left Roc soon after, traveling abroad to meet different sects that had formed in other countries. The sons and grandsons of the original leaders elected themselves into power, mostly through coercion and fear. Some years later, the trouble began again.

"Ten years after your disappearance, according to my records, the castle manifested from the fog. I am not sure how the fog figures in to this, but according to the peasants I was able to speak with, the castle simply appeared out of the fog on the very anniversary of your disappearance. One moment, the castle was not there, and the next it had appeared as if it had always been. And it was at this time that I became aware of myself again. Until this point, I do not remember where or what I was."

"How did you die?" I asked. Dread filled me after I asked, the smell of decay was so strong all around me. I could vividly see Edward's dead body now, lying on a dais surrounded by white flowers, his eyes open so wide he could have still been alive. I couldn't even remember that it was my father's memory anymore, nor could I seem to remember that I'd never been to Edward's funeral.

"I was burnt in the fire," he said softly. "They burnt the castle, you see. I could not leave the library, Sire... I could not... I could not." He rested his hand on the page and looked at me imploringly. "You must understand; this place is my life. I could never leave, not after all your family has done for me. I could never leave your history to burn with all these books. I tried to save them, I tried to save them from the fire, but everything burned anyway." His eyes were wide now, too similar to the death image in my mind for comfort.

"Edward, I wish you had survived," I whispered. "I wish you were still alive right now. You are more important to me than any book in the world."

"I could not, I simply could not," he said, a little horrified by my statement. "But do not worry about me, I saved one book. I saved one book from the fire with my own flesh." As he spoke, he stroked the pages of the red book. I realized then, staring at him petting the book as if it were a lover; he had died for that book. He had died for that book. I felt so sick and so angry that I leapt to my feet and threw the armchair into the fireplace. The chair made a resounding crash against the dusty fireplace and the clock on the mantel toppled over and exploded on the floor. Edward smiled wider, watching me systematically destroy the room.

I stopped and fell to my knees on the floor, panting.

I looked around, feeling slightly surprised. I felt like I'd just woken up and someone else had been wrecking the room. Edward was still smiling at me.

"There is nothing to be so angry about," he said gently. "It isn't so bad, being a ghost. The others carried on much as if nothing had happened at all. There were parties that I could not describe to you, scandals and tragedies so intense that everyone whispered about them for days. It is only when the exterminator came that we had problems."

"Exterminator?" I said. My voice was so calm I thought someone else had spoken.

"Yes," Edward said. "Eighty years after your disappearance, on the anniversary yet again, the People's Republic returned. They had grown far stronger since that day they stormed the castle. Many of the original members had been succeeded by their sons and grandsons. The arrogant tyrants forgot what their fathers had fought so hard for. They are back-stabbing, thoughtless pigs. They came to the castle and demanded we leave, claiming that the new republic would be built inside the castle as a symbol of their might over the old monarchy. They claimed it was what you would have wanted, having been martyred by it the way you were."

"Nonsense," I said. "Stupid..."

"Naturally, we knew that. We had no intention of going anywhere, but they were clever. They brought a ghost exterminator. They moved everyone to the library to get rid of us. When it was clear we could no longer leave this area, they tried moving into the castle. Thus far, they have had only minor success."

"I didn't see too many people," I said, thinking of the people living in my castle. I thought of New-Guy Rue and Joseph, and Pinky-Ring Harold and Ghost-Man. I felt hot with rage, like I was going to explode. "Why haven't I seen more people in the castle?"

"You know the secret passages within the castle," Edward said. "They do not. Besides, many of their wives hate it here, saying it's too quiet, too haunted. They are terrified of raising their families here. They don't stay, if they can help it. There are many servants still loyal to us who encourage such terror and do their best to make the castle unbearable."

"I'm sorry, Edward," I said. "I'm sorry for everything. If I hadn't run away that night... I was so stupid, such a coward."

"Sire, you couldn't have known what would happen," he said. "The rebels were waiting for an excuse, any excuse, to attack the castle; it had nothing to do with you at all. If anything, you would have been killed yourself if you had been here. There is nothing any of us could have done to prevent this. Now, please tell me what happened to you in the Widow's Lake. It is the only piece of information I am missing."

"What? Oh... the Lake. There isn't much to tell," I said. I felt so tired, thinking of all the tragedy I'd left in my wake.

"Please Sire, for the book," he said. I sighed and leaned forward, rubbing my face.

"Okay, Edward, okay. I'll tell you everything I know," I said.

I told him all that I could remember of the party and

the following events, including my conversation with the Skull Juggler by the side of the lake and the strange reaction I'd received from Geoffrey and Carlyle. All the while, I wondered only about one thing: what the hell am I going to do now?

Interlude
The Disenchanted King

Once, when the First Necromancer walked the Earth during one of his many adventures, he found a castle filled with ghosts. These particular spirits were so powerful and angry that no sun shone on their desolate home. Rain fell unceasingly from the sky as the gods wept for those poor souls trapped within and they felt deep sadness thinking that nothing could be done to help. It was at the urging of the gods that the First Necromancer went to this place.

The First Necromancer came to the castle and demanded admittance and hospitality for himself and his companion, the First Priestess of the Seventh God. The doorman allowed them entry after many hours and when they entered the castle, all manner of frightening creatures came to the First Necromancer. Old ghosts, new ghosts, sad ghosts, angry ghosts. All begged for release from this hell. A great curse had been placed upon them, they told the First Necromancer, which trapped them in the castle. So long as their king slept, they said, they would forever remain trapped.

The ruler of these ghosts was a good and noble king, although he was plagued by his own sin for drink and women. The Queen, who was a witch, cast a spell on her husband for him to sleep forever so that she might gaze upon his face whenever she chose. The ghosts wished to be free but they did not know how to escape without waking their king, and they did not know how to do this either.

The First Necromancer used his great magic to wake the king from his slumber and allowed the ghosts to leave the castle. The First Priestess of the Seventh God prayed for their safe journey to the Gray Fields and she prayed too for the King and his wife, the wicked Queen.

Upon discovering that her spell had been undone, the Queen flew into a terrible rage and fought with the King, trapping him in a silver cage so that she could put him under another spell. The First Priestess saw this and sacrificed herself in the King's stead so that the King could escape. Seeing this, the First Necromancer destroyed the wicked Queen with a death spell.

The First Necromancer protected his companion for seven days and seven nights while she slept, guarding her against all manner of evil spirits. When she awoke, she had gained great Knowledge of the Gods and Their ways.

It is for this reason that every year, the Priestesses of the Seventh God go into a deep sleep and return from the land of the Gods with great Knowledge.

- 13 -
Disenchanted

"This is all amazing," Edward said excitedly once I'd finished recounting my lengthy tale. I hadn't realized how much had happened to me until Edward asked me to describe everything in such excruciating detail. "Everything you have said is such a fascinating representation of magic so mysterious, even our most skilled scholars have not uncovered even a piece of what you have described here..." he paused, although not for the reason I thought.

"I'm glad my information was so helpful," I said tiredly. When Edward didn't respond, I looked up from my slouched position on his desk. Edward was staring at someone behind me. I felt a chill go up my spine when I realized that whoever it was, he (or she) was not alive.

"What did I tell you about trespassers, Edward," the smooth, cultured voice of my mother said by my ear. I'd thought I was prepared to hear that voice. How wrong I was.

I wanted to run screaming from the room. Up until this point, I could almost convince myself that none of it was real. If I squinted my eyes hard enough, Edward looked like he always had – tall, pale, and in desperate need of the outdoors. It was the same with Abigail. I hadn't seen a body, it didn't have to be real. Abigail was one of those people that simply existed, like the forest, like the sky. For her to be gone... it was too strange to wrap my mind around the concept of her death. She'd been so young the last time I'd seen her, far too young to be someone's mother, certainly too young to die.

This moment would change things. This would be acid to my denial, the wonderful story Edward told so eloquently being a mask for that denial. The reality of seeing someone so familiar would hit me harder then anything else had, and I knew it. I wanted to run but I stayed where I was. Whatever else might have happened, I couldn't escape now. She was my mother. She was Mom. I wasn't going to run from Mom.

When I worked up the nerve to look at her, I noted that she didn't look as I had expected. She was older now, with a few delicate wrinkles around her mouth from the persistent frown she'd worn in life and her hair was done in a different way. What I hadn't expected was that the face and hair were attached to the severed head she carried under her arm. That's right, she was carrying her head under her arm, as if it was a purse. It was a jarring sight and I tried not to change my facial expression as I stared down at her hip.

"Who do you think you..." she stopped. Her eyes widened and she lifted her head in both hands, putting the eyes closer to me. I gagged and fell back against the desk, knocking over some books. I grabbed my mouth to keep from vomiting, closing my eyes to block out the image. From this angle I could see the severed flesh around her throat and a bit of white spine dangling underneath. When I could open my eyes again, I stared fixedly at her face, specifically her eyes. She stared back at me with the same look she wore whenever something unexpected came up and ruined everything for her; an expression so familiar, it made me feel even more disconcerted.

"Christopher," she whispered. Slowly she drew her head back and hugged it to her chest. "I thought you were dead."

"I thought you were alive," I said when I could speak. "I didn't know... what happened."

"Insolent child," she whispered, her frown deepening. "You just disappeared, didn't you? You allowed all this misery to happen because you didn't care what would happen to me. You planned it with them!" I could guess who "them" was, something that only made me angrier and more frustrated with my situation.

"I've been trapped in the Widow's Lake for a hundred years, Mother," I growled. "I didn't have a choice about coming home. I only just escaped from there to find out that everything I've ever known and cared about is dead, and in the most grotesque way possible. Forgive me if I'm a little angry to see you!"

"Trapped?" she said, her eyebrows rising. It was just like her to forget what I'd just said, a bitter voice said in my head. At the same time, I was so glad to see her I couldn't think of anything really bad to say. I just stared at her, forcing back emotions that threatened to make me start screaming all over again.

"It is now all written," Edward said carefully. Mother opened her mouth to snap at him but a loud crash from outside made us all jerk around quickly.

I edged away from the door, trying to control my racing heart. Get a grip, get a grip, I thought to myself. I thought back to my spying in the corridor and realized that someone must have seen me. I'd been careless, thinking the meeting had been boring. After everything Edward had told me, however, I wished I'd stayed and listened to the whole thing. As bureaucratic as they'd seemed, as slow as they'd seemed, it was their forefathers who had killed everyone in the castle. They were the most dangerous people in the castle and I'd sauntered away mocking them. I felt ill, thinking of how stupid I was.

Edward ducked through the wall and watched something happen outside. He returned soon after and put a finger to his lips, motioning for silence. Mother scowled and drifted beside me uneasily. Edward motioned quietly to the red book and mimicked picking it up. I lifted it, wincing at the scraping sound it made on the wood. There was another crash from outside and a terrified shriek, then a great deal of shouting started.

Edward motioned at me again and pointed to the fireplace. I kicked aside the wreckage of my earlier temper tantrum and crouched under the chimney. Mother huffed and stuck her head through the wall to talk to me.

"You can't leave!" she said.

"Your Majesty, he cannot stay here," Edward whispered urgently. He shouldn't have bothered, with all the noise I'd just made clearing the chimney.

"Why not?" Mother hissed. "I have not seen him in a hundred years and you want him to leave, now that he's finished helping you write in that stupid book!"

"If he is alive now, or at least still able to walk and command his own mind," Edward said quickly, eyeing the door, "then his purpose cannot be to remain trapped here forevermore, not under the control of the People's Republic." Mother sucked in a sharp breath and hissed, jerking when there was a loud crash just beyond the door.

"Is it them?" she said in a dangerous voice I'd never heard her use before. "Is it those murderers?"

"Yes, it's them," Edward said impatiently. "The guards are fighting them though. Geoffrey was smart; he got reinforcements when he left. They won't be able to fight back for long, judging by the sounds outside. Christopher, hurry up."

"He doesn't have to leave," Mother said. "I command you to stop him!"

Edward stubbornly persisted, "You don't think they would want to control him? If they've already heard that he's here, don't you think they won't stop at just finding him? No, he cannot remain. We must help him leave this place before they realize where he is."

"Where do you suggest he go?" she whispered scathingly. As they were arguing, I stuck my hand above me into the sharp crevices of the chimney, searching with my fingers for the secret latch that would open a passage on the other side of the room. The dust clung to my hands and made finding the subtle catch nearly impossible.

"The answer awaits him outside of this place," Edward said in a stage whisper. "There is some task he must accomplish away from the castle, otherwise he would not be here now. He would have appeared in the castle eighty years ago, like we all did, if he was a ghost."

"No," Mother said sharply. "I have not seen him nearly long enough and you shall not take him away from me now! Not when I have already lost him once..." she stopped and turned her head around to press against her chest. The gesture was so gruesome and, at the same time, so vulnerable that I couldn't look away. I ducked my head to look at her, fingers still searching the wall.

She cried, hugging her own head and when she spoke, her words were muffled by her chest. "Christopher, Christopher, my baby... you were gone... dead... I couldn't keep grieving, I couldn't. To lose you both."

"Mother... please don't cry," I said, feeling ashamed for yelling at her before. She hadn't seen me in a century and I come back bitching. My fingers stilled on the wall and I drew them back. Without stopping to think, I reached out to comfort her. My hand touched her shoulder as the shouting reached a fevered pitch outside with the occasional clash of metal hitting metal. I could just see torchlight flickering under the door.

Mother slowly turned her head and stared at me wide-eyed. I didn't understand why she was so surprised until I remembered – she was a ghost. I shouldn't have been able to touch her.

She was so shocked, she dropped her head. It vanished before it hit the ground and then it materialized on top of her shoulders and she changed. It was so subtle; I could barely watch it happen, like watching a tree grow. Her skin shifted from the ash gray it had been to a soft pink. Her hair softened from the wire-like insanity it was before, becoming the controlled rush of gold I'd remembered from before, and she breathed in so deeply that her entire body shook.

Watching this happen, I realized something. I'd forgotten what life had been like before my father's death, when Mother used to smile at me the way she was now, as if she was proud of something I had said or done. I'd forgotten how her face lit up from the inside out when she smiled, how her face had changed after his death, lined with worry lines. And I felt so stupid that I'd thought she might have had anything to do with his murder. I nearly kicked myself when I thought of it. I saw into her mind then, as I touched her shoulder, and time slowed.

I saw the way she had cried when I was gone, cried until there were no more tears left in her. I saw her depression each day, her indecision over whether to marry, watched my half-sister's birth, watched her lose her mind when baby Anne was taken from her, watched her spit in the face of her executioner, felt the sharp pain in my neck, and then she was gone.

I blinked and looked around but she wasn't in the room anymore. Someone shouted outside and something large rammed into the door so hard, it nearly fell off its hinges.

"Mother?" I murmured, ignoring the commotion. Edward was scribbling desperately in the book, ignoring me. "Mom?" I poked my head up the chimney but found nothing. Scrambling around the room, I nearly tore the desk off the floor but I knew, I just knew, she wasn't there. She wasn't anywhere in the room, I realized. Whatever I'd done, she was gone now. I felt numb.

"Edward? Edward, where is she? What happened? What did I do?" I looked around the room more frantically, my hands shaking. Edward did not seem to hear me, something that only made me more panicked and angry. How could he keep writing in that stupid book when I'd just done something to my mother? Something, I had the sinking feeling, I couldn't undo?

What was I supposed to do now? The door was breaking, people were coming in. What would become of me now? What did the People's Republic of Roc plan to do with me, their old king? I was a threat, I knew, to their very way of being. None of their plans would have succeeded, at least not so quickly, if I hadn't disappeared at exactly the right moment? They would probably pretend to need me... they might even give me some remote amount of power to rule. What did it matter though, if I was dead? They would figure that out soon enough. I couldn't have just vanished from the castle for one hundred years without some interference from magic. Would they lock me up somewhere and experiment on me? What would become of me?

I grabbed Edward's arm in my panic, just as I'd touched my mother's shoulder. I wanted to feel something familiar but, just as before, something strange happened. Edward gasped when I touched him, his eyes jerking up to meet mine. He fumbled on the desk and grabbed the little stone, the piece of his wife's gravestone, and smiled.

"Thank you, Christopher. Thank you," he said as

he too disappeared. The rock dropped from the air and when it landed on the floor, the entire castle began to shake like a firework about to explode. I gasped and grabbed the side of the desk, holding on as tightly as I could. The walls disappeared, becoming black and crooked. The floor dissolved under me but, as if it had never been, the library was no more.

Between two breaths, I was standing inside of a strange room I'd never seen before with Edward's book clutched tightly in my hands. I ran to the door and kicked it open, desperate to understand what had happened.

The castle was gone. I stared wide-eyed at what remained in its place, the ashes and scorched earth. There was some greenery here and there and a deer grazed on the far side, but otherwise there was nothing there. I looked up at the building I was in, trying to understand what I'd done.

The building I was standing in, this was the strange building I'd seen when I first came out of the forest after I'd escaped the Widow's Lake, the one that had seemed so odd, as if it needed to be isolated on a tall hill. Looking around now at the sparse landscape, the cold building must have looked perfect right next to the pile of ashes that had been the castle. The stables, I noted, were no longer there. The strange super-imposed image was gone, leaving the strange building very alone and very real.

"That's an interesting piece of work," a voice said from inside the building, directly behind me. I whirled around and froze, noticing for the first time that I hadn't been alone. The Skull Juggler sat on a coffin I hadn't noticed before, swinging his leg lazily. "It was a very complex spell to untangle but you found the source. Congratulations."

"What?" I said dumbly. "I didn't do anything! I... What happened to all of them, to all of the ghosts?"

"They've moved on, I expect," he said, eyeing me. He wore a black cloak over his traveling clothes, his eyes on the book in my hands. "Or perhaps their souls were attracted back to the book, just as before. There is no way to tell with these things. Sometimes we must rely on Providence to let things happen as they will." He said the last part as if it were some sort of morbid joke he didn't think I'd understand.

"Why?" I mumbled, unsure what I was even asking.

"None of this would have happened if that stupid boy hadn't tried to take the book from the castle grounds, not that he'll ever know it was entirely his fault. Anyway, the point is that your ghosts have finished their business on this plane of existence and are gone to who-knows-where," he said with a dismissive wave of his hand.

"Oh," I said faintly. In the back of my mind, I remembered some little piece of information about ghosts. They were the memories of people who had not been able to finish whatever they felt was important and necessary during their lifetimes and so, to finish that work, they remained in spirit form. When that business was finished, the spirit could rest or move on to the Gray Fields. Was that what had happened? Mother and Edward had seemed so happy when they disappeared. Had

I somehow done the same thing to all the other ghosts? Who else had I spiritually "helped?"

"You don't have to worry about the living ones," the Skull Juggler said as he slid off the coffin and walked towards me. "They're all safe and sound in the town square. I can't tell you what a good laugh I had, watching them scramble about after appearing there. Made up for all this damned waiting."

"Waiting?" I mumbled. My mind, so foggy before, allowed me at last to see him clearly. "You were waiting for me?"

"Of course," he said, brushing dust from his shoulder. "We have work to do together. I can't very well do it without you, now can I?" I stared at him, piecing it together. I remembered what Edward had said, about having some other work to do, my own unfinished business. If I was supposed to move on in death like the ghosts obviously had, I would have disappeared with the castle. Was this my future? Was this what he'd meant? Was the Skull Juggler's presence here, now, not a coincidence but a planned sequence of events?

"Geoffrey..." I began. "He was in the castle, waiting for me... there was shouting..."

"He is perfectly safe. I told you, everyone who was alive in the castle is fine," he said. "I am sure he is perfectly safe."

I didn't know what to feel. Part of me felt that I'd just lost them all over again, and yet another part of me was convinced that this whole thing had been a dream. I thought that, maybe, I'd wake up and find out that my father had died only yesterday. I'd go to the death festivities with Mother and spend my time making snide comments about my guests with Richard. I thought maybe, just maybe, I'd wake up, still alive, still king, and still engaged to Evelyn. All of those thoughts seemed so far away, I couldn't even touch them anymore. I felt like a blank piece of paper with a pen poised above it, ready to write something down.

"Oh," I finally managed to say. I looked down at the book in my hands, imagining how Edward must have curved his body around it, how he must have thought of his dead wife, and how much he must have wished to be reunited with her. I felt sick looking at the book in my hands. I walked past the Skull Juggler to the coffin and kicked the lid off so hard that it clanged loudly on the floor.

There was nothing inside but a metal plaque with my name on it and the birth and death dates. This must have been my tomb, I realized. I looked up without thinking and scanned the tomb. There, hidden somewhat, was a life-size statue of me. I couldn't stomach looking at it for long, it was a whole level of creepy I'd never experienced before, but I knew now why it seemed that everyone knew what I looked like. How appropriate that this should be my final resting place, a place so cold that even I felt disturbed by its morbidity. I placed the book on top of the plaque in my coffin, rubbing my sweaty hands on my pants. I went carefully around to the coffin lid and tried to lift it.

The Skull Juggler was on the other side instantly and helped me lift it back onto the coffin. There were morbid designs etched into the stone, skulls and bones, perhaps a reflection of what the mason-worker had thought I'd look like after I'd decayed for a few years. I stared at the coffin for a moment, thinking about all I had learned in the castle and all that I had lost, and then looked up at the man who might have very well orchestrated the whole thing. He stared back at me without any sign of fear or surprise.

"What's your name?" I said, surprising myself with how angry I sounded.

"Andreas," he said. The Skull Juggler Andreas. It didn't sound quite as formidable as I had thought but I wasn't going to say that. I wasn't going to say much for a while. I rubbed a hand through my hair and took a deep breath.

"It's a pleasure to meet you, Andreas. I'm Christopher. Now let's get the hell out of here," I said.

He grinned and made a sweeping bow, motioning for the door.

About the Author

Natalia Locatelli started writing at the age of 11, although the world will probably never see those early struggles to find her voice. When she was 15 years old, she started writing fanfiction under the pen name "Amber Evans Potter," including but not limited to such subjects as Harry Potter, Sailor Moon, the Phantom of the Opera, and many others.

By the age of 17, she knew she wanted to write professionally and began her shift from fanfiction to the world of original writing. She thinks the world of those who helped her find her writing voice, especially the fanfiction readers who loyally followed her stories (which are still online). She even has some friends still out there in cyberspace who have sworn to write *Skull Juggler* fanfiction to amuse her.

Now 20 years old, a senior at the University of Miami, and majoring in English Literature, Natalia is looking forward to an enduring writing career. She has several projects planned in the immediate future, the biggest of which is the next book in Christopher's journey with the Skull Juggler.

She has edited such works as *Leading Under Pressure: Maximize Your Health While Building Your Wealth* and the provocative *Alpha Female: Leader of a Pack of Bitches – Winning Strategies to Become an Outstanding Leader* by her overachieving mom. Natalia has been ordained, in the name of familial responsibility (after all, she is Italian), to write *Alpha Female in Training*. In addition, she is involved in another family project with her Grammy-award winning uncle (yes, she knows just how insanely gifted her family is, don't rub it in) and her mom, called Mystic Accord. For more information about Natalia's upcoming projects, visit her website at www.NataliaLocatelli.com.

For more information on the upcoming *Skull Juggler* series, go to www.SkullJuggler.com.